Frank Lebby Stanton

Songs of the Soil

Frank Lebby Stanton

Songs of the Soil

ISBN/EAN: 9783337248864

Printed in Europe, USA, Canada, Australia, Japan

Cover: Foto ©Andreas Hilbeck / pixelio.de

More available books at **www.hansebooks.com**

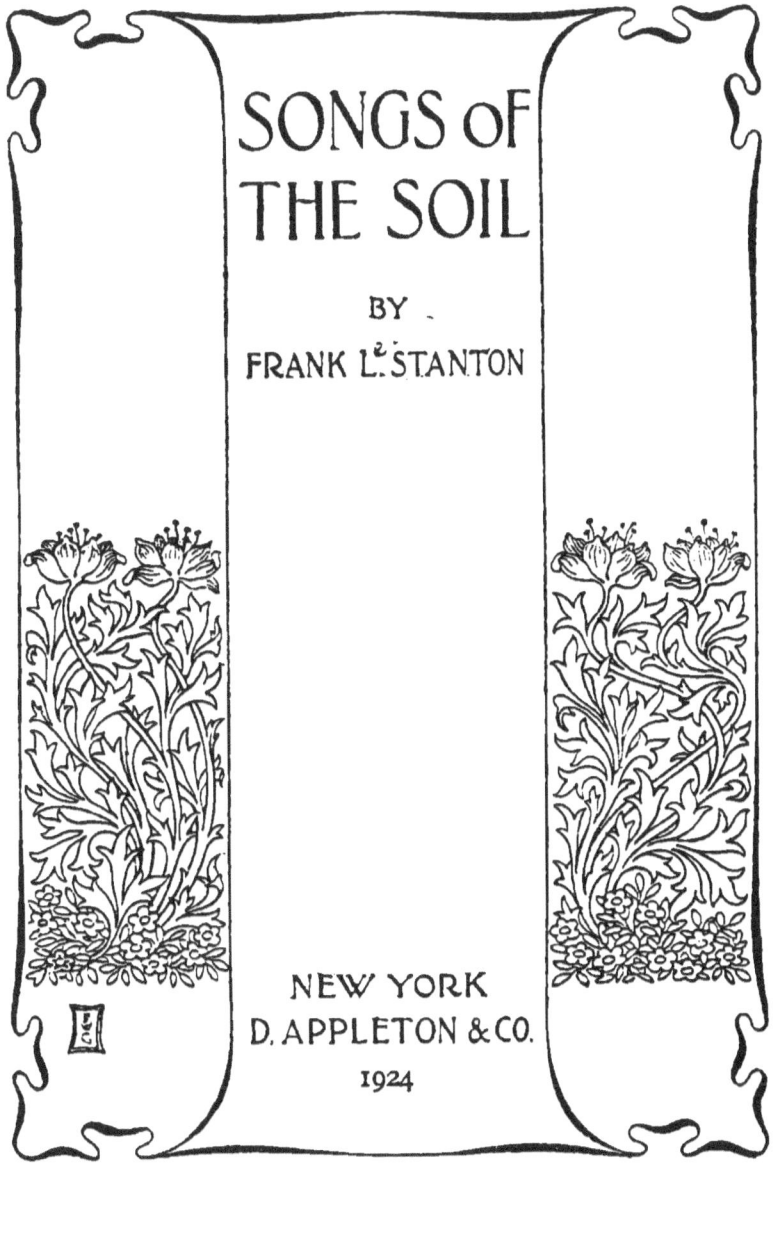

SONGS of THE SOIL

BY
FRANK L. STANTON

NEW YORK
D. APPLETON & CO.
1924

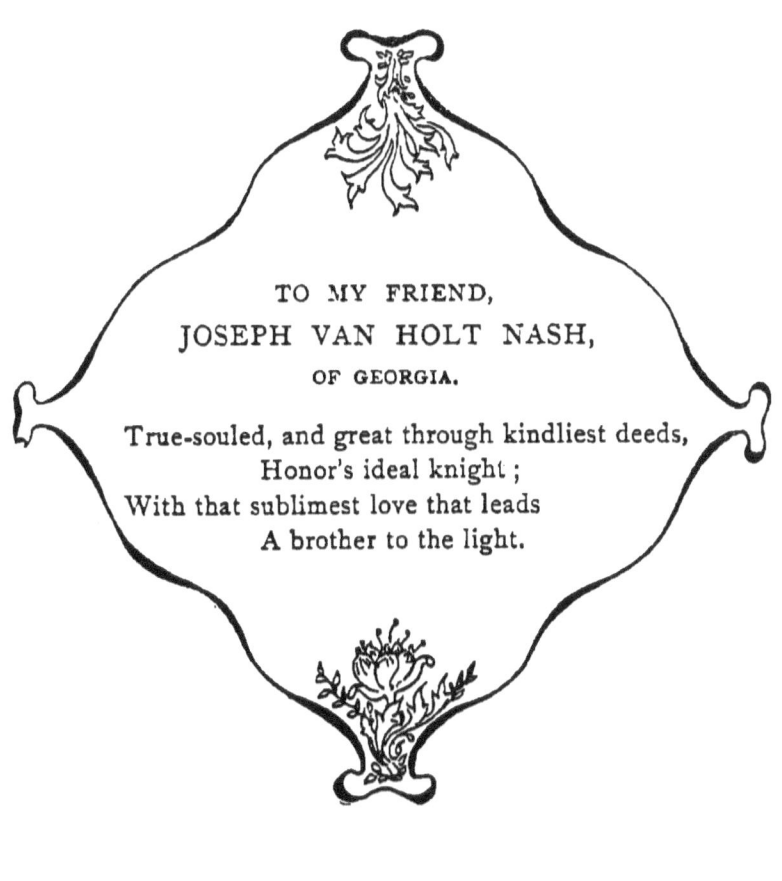

TO MY FRIEND,

JOSEPH VAN HOLT NASH,

OF GEORGIA.

True-souled, and great through kindliest deeds,
Honor's ideal knight ;
With that sublimest love that leads
A brother to the light.

PREFACE.

In some important respects the poetry of Mr. Stanton presents a phenomenon that is well worth the attention of those who are interested in the development of that branch of American literature that finds voice in the South. In the first place, the writings of no American poet have achieved such wide popularity, if we are to measure popularity by the daily and weekly newspapers of the country, or by the interest which makes itself manifest in private correspondence, or by the appreciation which betrays itself in the irresistible desire of composers, professionals and amateurs, to give a musical setting to the poems. These manifestations are not by any means confined to this country. In England the literary weeklies have seized upon the poems as something new and striking. The result of this is that the phenome-

nal popularity of Mr. Stanton's verses in this
country finds a hearty echo in Great Britain.

A prominent English author, writing to Mr.
Stanton, says : " Your poems are gaining reputa-
tion for you in England. The note of hope that
you are singing is one that has been unheard for
years." This remark, casually made, possesses
unusual significance. We know a great deal more
than our fathers knew. Profound sophistication
is the order of the day. We see it rankly devel-
oped in the stories that women are writing. Evo-
lution has become revolution. Sham culture,
brought to book (to speak literally), confesses that
the beastliness of the primal ape remains pretty
near the surface of things. The poets flutter
somewhat higher. That which is insipid vulgarity
in prose blossoms into pessimism in verse. In the
magazines and in the newspapers it is the same.
Knowing too much, we know nothing! There is
no future any more. Everything is hopeless
gloom. That which we have not already lost we
shall presently lose, and there is no remedy. In
fact, no remedy is necessary. There is nothing to

be done but to eat cold muffins and drink tea, and make ourselves as comfortable as possible under the circumstances.

It is in the midst of these conditions that the voice of a singer away down South, in the provincial regions, makes itself heard. It is a bold voice, too, for it persists in singing night and day, neither seeking nor avoiding an audience. If the world listens, well and good: if not, pleasant dreams to all for the sake of old times! But the world listens. The newspapers pick up the songs and send them far and wide, till the voice of the singer is carried over the continent and into the isles of the sea. People say, "Who is this man that goes on singing day after day as if there had never been a singer in the world before him?" They find that he has the root of the matter in him, and so they listen gladly.

It will be interesting to note what the critics— the apostles of culture—will say of Mr. Stanton's verses. We shall hear, no doubt, that they lack finish, that too little attention has been paid to the demands of literary art. It is so easy to talk about literary art, and so hard to know what it is! It is such a dreadful thing in and of itself that those who venture into print for the first time are in quite a stew until somebody they have never heard of before discovers for them whether they understand anything about literary art. And they are old and gray in the business before they discover for themselves that the only true literary art is the atmosphere of individuality which each mind with a message creates for itself.

As for Mr. Stanton's poems, they have all been struck off in the heat and hurry of newspaper work, not as things apart, but as a matter of course. As one of the writers on the Atlanta Constitution, he has a department which he calls "Just from Georgia." He has chosen to preface this department with at least one original piece of verse every morning. But frequently he writes four and five poems a day, not because he is expected to write them, but because they are waiting to be written. The marvel of this fluency is that the result should be so significant, that the earnestness and simplicity of the note he strikes should be so manifest. His readers have no need to be told that whether he blithely sings of youth and love or, more seriously, of life and hope, he is not playing with his theme.

In a period that fairly reeks with the results of a sham culture that is profoundly ignorant of the verities of life, and a sham philosophy that worships mere theories, it surely is something to find a singer breathing unceremoniously into Pan's pipes and waking again the woodland echoes with snatches of song that ring true to the ear, because they come straight from the heart. We were told a while ago by one of the sophisticated brethren that the poet of the future would come to us singing of science. The dreaded possibility still lies before us. Meanwhile, here is one with the dew of morning in his hair, who looks on life and the promise thereof and finds the prospect joyous. Whereupon, he lifts up his voice and speaks to the heart: and lo! here is Love, with nimble feet and sparkling eyes; and here is Hope, fresh risen from his sleep; and here is Life made beautiful again.

JOEL CHANDLER HARRIS.

CONTENTS.

(xi)

SONGS OF THE SOIL.

A SONG OF SUMMER-TIME.

O summer-time in Georgy—I love to sing your
praise!
Though I've got no voice fer singin', it's a tune I
love to raise
When the birds is pantin', chantin', an' jest rantin'
roun' the rills,
With the juice o' ripe blackberries jest a-drippin'
from their bills!

O summer-time in Georgy, when through leaves o'
green an' brown
The dew that smells o' violets comes twinklin',
tinklin' down

On the wild an' wavin' grass that feels the sunbeam as it slips,
An' the dusty lily puckers up its white an' thirsty
lips!

O summer-time in Georgy, with the glory in the
dells,
Where the rich an' rainy incense from the fresh-
'nin' shower swells,
An' crost the bars to twinklin' stars float twilight's
fare-you-wells
In the lowin' o' the cattle an' the tinklin' o' the
bells!

O summer-time in Georgy, when nigh the listenin'
vine,
Where the purple mornin'-glory an' the honeysuckle twine.
The whip-poor-wills was singin' their notes o' love
an' bliss,
An' to my lips was clingin' the lips I loved to
kiss!

Stay, like a dream o' beauty, while deares' dreams
    depart,

An' rain your honey-sweetness in showers roun'
    my heart !

Pshaw ! I'm gittin' so soft-hearted, my eyes kin'
    hardly see :

O summer-time in Georgy ! You're the best o'
    times to me !

NIGHT IN THE SOUTH.

Here in the deep, June dark,
    Laden with odors of the rose excessive,
Where not a star ray strikes the oaks to mark
    Their glooms impressive,

I tilt my rustic chair—
    The smoke from my Havana upward wreathing,
And o'er the rolling of the world I hear
    The great Night breathing!

The night that has no art
    To hide her grief; with dim-draped arms ex-
        tended,
She waits to welcome to her widowed heart
    The moonrise splendid.

And yet—so still is all
    That if a bird's nest slipped its airy tether

(4)

There would be sound and feeling in the fall
  Of one light feather !

The rills that brawled all day,
  Now with the tumbled pebbles make no
    wrangle ;
The wind seems weary and has lost its way
  In vines a-tangle.

In vines where odorous swings
  The honeysuckle, o'er the senses stealing ;
Where humming-birds have brushed with beau-
    teous wings
  The wild grapes reeling !

Night ! and the South ! and June !
  Silence—and yet, the sound of many voices !
And now, dashed down the darkness, tune on tune,
  And melody rejoices !

Clear through the awakened night
  The music rushes—all the joy-bells ringing ;
And every leaf is trembling with delight
  Born of that singing !

It is as if a word
　Had flashed from God—aweary of the quiet;
The soul of Music in a mocking-bird
　In maddest riot!

Night! and the South! and June!
　The wind awakes; the river sings its story;
Up from the black hills climbs the brimming moon
　In full-blown glory!

The distant hills grow bright:
　The oaks stand clear; the loneliest nook un-
　　covers;
The keen vines listen for the footsteps light
　Of whispering lovers!

A flash on fields and streams,
　And *one* bird's song tumultuous and tender;
And then—the languor of melodious dreams,
　And earth all splendor!

LYNCHED.

The tramp of horse adown a sullen glen ;
Dark forms of stern, unmerciful masked men :

A clash of arms, a cloven prison door,
And a man's cry for mercy ! . . . Then high o'er

The barren fields, dim outlined in the storm,
The swaying of a lifeless human form.

And close beside, in horror and affright,
A widowed woman wailing to the night.

THE CALL OF THE REAPERS.

I know that it is reaping-time in all the fields of
    Lee ;
I can hear the reapers singing o'er the meadows,
    calling me :
" And wherefore come you not to-day to reap the
    golden grain ? "
But I'll never see the fields of Lee, nor reap with
    them again.

" And wherefore come you not to-day ? " they cry
    across the wheat ;
" And wherefore come you not ? " the winds are
    chiming low and sweet ;
And far and near sweet sounds I hear from over
    mount and main ;
But I shall not see the fields of Lee, nor reap in
    them again.

"Oh, wherefore come you not? The hand of
    Summer decks the sod ;
The world is like a picture where the harvests
    smile to God ;
There's yet a late white rose for you in valley and
    in plain."
But I shall not see the fields of Lee, where blooms
    that rose, again.

"Ah, wherefore come you not? The doves have
    left their woodland nests,
With the silver sunrise gleaming on their downy,
    tender breasts ;
And they're calling to you soft: 'Come home!'"
    But all their calls are vain ;
For I shall not hear the birds sing in the fields of
    Lee again.

Oh, comrades, cease your crying, as ye reap in
    fields of Lee ;
Ye have there so many reapers there is never
    need of me !

Oh, doves, leave not your nests, nor call in tender
    tones and vain,
To him who hears, with falling tears, but can not
    come again.

Reap on, ye men and maids of Lee; for ye that
    sow must reap ;
And I am reaping far away while ye your vigils
    keep ;
But there is no song upon my lips, nor golden is
    the grain,
And I shall not see the fields of Lee, nor reap
    with you again !

WHAT BOTHERS HIM.

There ain't so much o' pleasure
  In fishin' South in May,
Or any other blessed month—
  No matter what they say !

Because the river bank is green ;
  The grass is soft an' deep,
An' where the shady willows lean
  A feller falls to sleep.

An' jest when he begins to nod
  'Longside his empty cup,
A fish comes jerkin' at his rod
  An' always wakes him up !

(11)

ME AN' MARY.

There's a lot o' fun in livin' an' a lot o' joy in
life
When a feller's got a sweetheart—'fore he's thinkin' of a wife;
An' sayin' that remin's me that I lived on honeycomb
When Mary did the milkin' an' I drove the cattle
home.

I was mighty clost to twenty, an' was kinder shy
an' green,
An' the writin' in the Bible put down Mary seven-
teen;
I'd been thinkin' o' the city—bein' much inclined
to roam,
But somehow I liked the cattle, an' kept drivin' of
'em home.

You see, the cattle *knowed* me—been a-drivin' of
 em' so ;
An' Mary had to milk 'em at a certain time, you
 know !
An' when I'd think o' clerkin' an' leavin' o' the
 loam,
I'd wonder an' I *wonder* who would drive the
 cattle home.

But there warn't so much in farmin', or in drivin'
 cows to milk :
It kept me down to cotton-jeans an' Mary fur
 from silk ;
So I made my mind up *certain*, an' I packed my
 trunk to start ;
An' I kept a-sayin' *careless :* "It'll break nobody's
 heart."

I remember it was springtime—'bout the settin' o'
 the sun—
When I broke the news to Mary like 'twas jest the
 biggest fun !

But I noticed while she listened that the milkin'
    slowed—then stopped,
An' she looked acrost the meadows, an' her eyes—
    they kinder dropped!

An' I said: "I'm sorry, Mary, but the time is
    come to go:
I hate to leave the country, likin' all the *cattle*
    so!"
Then her eyes looked up an' met me, an' I felt
    the lightnin' strike
As the words come mighty tremblin': "Is the
    cattle all you like?"

Somethin' hit me! *thought* a minute, lookin' down
    into her eyes,
Wich was like a dream o' heaven, an' jest took in
    all the skies;
An' I felt myself a-shakin' like I'd struck a day in
    fall;
But I said it—drawin' clost to her: "*No, Mary,
    cows ain't all!*"

It was quicker'n *I* kin tell it, or than even the law
  allows,
But the milk drowned out the daisies, an' the
  calves got with the cows!
An' my arms was all aroun' her, an' my heart
  jumped out my vest,
An' my vote was fer the country, fer I liked the
  country best!

Warn't no milk on *that* plantation that evenin'—
  not a drop!
The cows got in the gyarden an' jest eat up half
  the crop!
But the food that *I* was feedin' on was sweet as
  honeycomb,
From the red, sweet lips o' Mary, as I kissed her
  goin' home!

I lost sight o' the city life, whatever it might
  be:
One acre in the country was enough, an' *more*, fer
  me!

An' I'm mixed up with the meadows, an' I never
    want to roam,
Fer Mary does the milkin' an' I drive the cattle
    home!

AN OLD BATTLEFIELD.

The softest whisperings of the scented South,
And rust and roses in the cannon's mouth.

And where the thunders of the fight were born,
The wind's sweet tenor in the tinkling corn.

With song of larks, low-lingering in the loam,
And blue skies bending over love and home.

But still the thought: Somewhere—upon the hills,
Or where the vales ring with the whip-poor-wills,

Sad, wistful eyes and broken hearts that beat
For the loved sound of unreturning feet;

And when the oaks their leafy banners wave,
Dream of the battle and an unmarked grave!

A LITTLE HAND.

Perhaps there are tenderer, sweeter things
  Somewhere in this sun-bright land;
But I thank the Lord for his blessings,
  And the clasp of a little hand.

A little hand that softly stole
  Into my own that day,
When I needed the touch that I loved so much
  To strengthen me on the way.

Softer it seemed than the softest down
  On the breast of the gentlest dove;
But its timid press and its faint caress
  Were strong in the strength of love!

It seemed to say in a strange, sweet way:
  "I love you and understand";

And calmed my fears as my hot, heart tears
  Fell over that little hand.

.   .   .   .   .   .

Perhaps there are tenderer, sweeter things
  Somewhere in this sun-bright land;
But I thank the Lord for his blessings,
  And the clasp of a little hand.

THE PICNIC AT SELINA.

That picnic at Selina—it covered lots o' groun';
There was women, men, an' hosses from fifteen
mile aroun',
An' fiddles squeaked an' brogans creaked the mer-
riest kind o' song,
An' 'twas " Balance to your pardners ! " and
" Swing ! " the whole day long.

'Twas a powerful sight o' pleasure jest to see the
fellers whirl
Them lovely forms in calico, with all their hair in
curl !
It was quite intoxicatin'; you could hear the
rafters ring,
Till the *old* men couldn't stand it, an' cut the
" pigeon wing " !

The old-time "double-shuffle" made the dust fly
    from their heels,
An' 'twas sich a jolly scuffle in the Old Virginny
    reels;
The young men jest a-sweatin', an' the rosy gals
    a-blowin'—
But they didn't mind the weather while they kept
    the fiddle goin'!

"It's jolly!" roared the rafters. "It's painful!"
    groaned the floor:
"It's dusty!" said the women, but they only
    danced the more;
An' the young men called it "stavin'," an' I reckon
    they was right,
Fer that old-time Georgia "breakdown" made the
    stars dance with delight!

All day the fiddle's music was ringin' wild an'
    sweet;
The nigger parson rolled it off an' kept time with
    his feet;

All day, with jest a breathin' spell 'long 'bout the
time o' noon,
The dancers kept in motion an' the fiddle kept in
tune.

An' then here come the dinner—table stretchin'
'way
Out yonder, till it dwindled to a *leetle* mist o'
gray :
There was punkins, there was pullets, all a-lookin'
o' their best ;
An' 'possums, an' pot licker, till a feller couldn't
rest !

An' everybody went fur 'em—jest made a dash
fer *all*,
Till them chickens o' the springtime wished they
hadn't hatched till fall !
An' the punkins kept agoin' as they come in
reach o' me,
An' I made them 'possums wonder how they ever
climbed a tree !

But good things can't last furever; the honey
  leaves the comb ;
An so, we had to be resigned to hitchin' up fer
  home ;
An', if I don't disremember, I was drivin' of a bay
On a zigzag road, an' huggin' of a widder all the
  way !

That picnic at Selina ! it ain't to be fergot !
Fer a feller felt as happy's if he owned a house
  an' lot !
An' thinkin' o' them women folks, all dressed up
  fit to kill,
I kin feel my heart agoin' like a old rice beater
  still !

There'll be good times at Selina in the happy days
  to be,
But never any times like that fer all the boys an'
  me ;
Fer the mem'ry o' that picnic—it'll live a hundered
  years,
An' I'll feel my old feet shufflin' when I climb the
  golden stairs !

FOR YOU.

For you, dear heart, the light—
  God's smile, where'er you be,
And if he will—the night,
  Only the night for me !

For you Love's own dear land
  Of roses, fair and free ;
And if you will—no hand
  To give a rose to me.

For you Love's dearest bliss
  In all the years to be ;
And if you will—no kiss
  Of any love for me.

Thankful to know you blest,
  When God your brow adorns
With the sweet roses of his rest,
  I thank him for the thorns !

DREAMING OF HOME.

I can't jest tell what's come to her, an' yet I think
    it's clear
That somethin's goin' wrong o' late—to see her
    settin' there
A-dreamin' in the doorway, with that look into
    her eyes,
As if they still was restin' on the fur-off fields an'
    skies.

She's always dreamin', dreamin' o' the life we left
    behind—
The cozy little cottage where the mornin'-glories
    twined ;
The roses in the garden—the yellow sunflowers
    tall ;
The violets—but she herself the sweetest flower
    o' all !

You see, she use' to set there in the mornin's—so
content;
The sunflowers follerin' the sun, no matter where
he went;
The brown bees sippin' honey an' a-buzzin' roun'
the place;
The roses climbin' up to her an' smilin' in her
face!

An' now, she can't fergit it; when I tell her:
" Little wife,
There ain't no use in grievin' fer that simple
country life,"
She twines her dear arms roun' my neck, an'
smilin' sweet to see,
She whispers: " We're so fur away from where we
use' to be! "

There ain't no use in chidin', or in sayin' words o'
cheer;
There's nothin' in this city life like she was use to
there,

Where preachin' come but once a month, an' street
    cars didn't run,
An' folks they told the time o' day by lookin' at
    the sun.

An' larks got up at peep o' day an' made the
    meadows ring !
I tell you, folks, when one's brought up to jest
    that sort o' thing,
It's hard to git away from it—old feelin's bound
    to rise
An' make a runnin' over in a woman's tender
    eyes !

So there she sets a-dreamin', till I git to dreamin',
    too ;
An' when her head drops on my breast and sleep
    falls like the dew
An' closes them bright eyes o' hers, once more we
    seem to be
In the old home where we'll rest some day to-
    gether—her an' me !

SLAIN.

Swiftly the shot from my rifle sped
To his heart, and he fell in the darkness—dead !

With never a struggle, never a sigh,
I saw my enemy bleed and die.

And now, I said, is my peace secure ;
I shall fear his hand and his hate no more.

The black night came with a stealthy pace
And shed the shadows over his face,

Hidden forever from mortal view :
And only God and the darkness knew !

But what would I barter of good and fair
To take the place of the dead man there,

As I face the future—the life to be,
With God and the darkness haunting me !

OLD TIMES IN GEORGY.

Old times in Georgy—them's the times fer me !
No times now like *them* times, an' ain't agoin' to
    be !
Long time 'fore the railroads an' steamboats
    blowin' free—
How I like to dream o' them—good old times to
    me !

Old times in Georgy — them's the times that
    make
My old eyes dance an' twinkle like sunshine on
    the lake ;
An' sometimes, too, they kinder bring feelin's 'kin
    to pain,
An' make my eyes run over like rivers full o'
    rain !

Old times in Georgy—can't fergit 'em *quite*—
Suns that made the daytime—stars that come at
    night ;
Oh ! but they was *good* times—country smilin'
    bright !
Everything was love then—everything was light.

Old times in Georgy—hear my old heart beat
When they come a-ringin' with their music sweet !
Dreamin' of 'em always, mountains, hills, an' dells,
They're like a sweet song's echo—a fur-off chime
    o' bells !

Old times in Georgy—they was sweet to know—
Old friends that loved us, friends that we loved so !
Seem to lost my way, now—ain't much left to
    see—
Them dear old times in Georgy is all life's got fer
    me !

THE OLD BRIGADE.

When Pearson sang "The Old Brigade," how all
   the boys kept time !
The muskets rattled once again, the cannon
   roared in rhyme ;
With shoulder close to shoulder still, again the
   charge they made,
With all the torn flags waving o'er the old
   Brigade !

When Pearson sang "The Old Brigade," 'twas
   " Forward—march !" and then—
The shouting of the captains and the rallying of
   the men !
The storming of the ramparts, and the battle,
   blade to blade—
Oh, the story and the glory of the old Brigade !

When Pearson sang " The Old Brigade," the boys
    kept time with sighs,
And something like a teary mist dimmed all their
    dreaming eyes ;
For lo ! the fight is ended, the rust is on each
    blade,
And the grass grows green forever o'er the old
    Brigade !

NOT MELANCHOLY DAYS.

These ain't the "melancholy days," no matter
    what they say!
There's more good fun in all the ways than's been
    there many a day!
The crackin' of the teamster's whip—the shoutin'
    of a boy
As the apples come a-tumblin' down—that's joy fer
    you—big joy!

These ain't the "melancholy days"—there's lots o'
    fun in sight;
The cool and bracin' mornin's, an' the big oak fires
    at night;
The hounds upon the rabbit's trail—the wild doves
    on the wing—
The maiden with the red lips, an' the lover with
    the ring!

These ain't the "melancholy days"—not much!
    they're full o' life,
An' you're thankful fer your sweetheart, an' you
    praise God fer your wife!
An' then, on general principles—in view of what
    he's givin'—
You shout a hallelujah fer the privilege o' livin'!

FALLEN ASLEEP.

Only a little dust—
    So small that a rose might hide it;
And I trust in God—or I try to trust,
    When I kneel in the dark beside it.

I kneel in the dark and say:
    I only dream that I weep;
She would not leave me and go away—
    She has only fallen asleep.

Fallen asleep, as oft
    She climbed to my heart to rest,
Her white arms twining my neck, as soft
    As down on a dove's sweet breast.

Tenderly—unawares,
    Sleep came in the waning light
And kissed her there on the twilight stairs
    That lead to the morning bright.

And that she will wake I know,
 And smile at a grief like this;
It could not be she would leave me so,
 With never a good-night kiss!

So I kneel in the dark and say:
 I only dream that I weep;
She would not leave me and go away—
 She has only fallen asleep.

FALL TIME.

Fall time in the country! ain't it out o' sight?
Hick'ry nuts a-droppin' an' fires blazin' bright!
'Taters in the ashes, apples on the shelf—
Pass aroun' the cider till you hardly know your-
   self!

Fall time in the country—people full o' life,
Everybody happy with his sweetheart or his wife!
Blue smoke from the cabins—up an' up it curls,
While we go a-rollickin' an' ridin' with the gyrls!

Fall time in the country—hardest time to beat!
Follerin' the banjer an' the fiddle with your feet;
Never nuthin' like it—happy day an' night,
Cider in the jimmyjohn an' fires blazin' bright!

THE THOUGHT OF YOU.

I care not whether the skies are blue,
  Or the clouds gloom black above me ;
A sweet thought comes with the thought of you—
  You love me, dear, you love me !

When the world is cold and its friendships few,
  And toil is a vain endeavor,
A sweet voice sings to my soul of you,
  And the world is sweet forever.

And love, my love, with the bright eyes true
  And the red lips kind with kisses,
There is no love like my love for you—
  No joy in the world like this is !

And whether the skies are dark or blue,
  With stars or storms above me,
My life will shine with the thought of you—
  You love me, dear, you love me !

WHEN JIM WAS DEAD.

When Jim was dead—
"It sarved him right," the neighbors said,
An' 'bused him fer the life he'd led,
An' him a-lyin' there at rest
With not one rose laid on his breast!
Hard words, an' lots o' them, they said
When Jim was dead.

"Jest killed hisself," "Too mean to live:"
They didn't have one word to give
In comfort, while they crowded near
An' looked on Jim a-lyin' there!
"Ain't any use to talk," they said:
"He's better dead!"

But suddently the room growed still,
While God's white sunshine seemed to fill

The dark place with a gleam o' life,
An' over him she bent—*Jim's wife!*
An' with her lips laid clost to his—
Jest like he knowed an' felt the kiss—
She sobbed—a touchin' sight to see:
" Oh ! Jim was always good to me ! "

I tell you, when *that* come to light
It kinder set the dead man right;
An' round the weepin' woman they
Throwed kindly arms o' love that day;
An' fallin' fast as hers, they shed
The tend'rest tears—when Jim was dead.

A SONG FOR HER.

Sing for her, mocking bird,
Your warm breast heaving in the sun-bright blos-
soms ;
Sing sweeter songs than we have ever heard,
Until the wild heart of the world is stirred,
And love wakes wondering in a thousand bosoms!

Sing for her, lark of dawn,
When on your breast the lofty light is gleaming !
Sing sweet, and bear the message on, and on—
Higher and higher, till the world is gone,
And at God's gates the melody is dreaming !

Sing for her, whip-poor-will,
Your sweet voice ringing from the twilight covers,
Where stars stream splendid over vale and hill ;
Sing sweet, until your melting notes shall thrill
And throng the wide, awakened world with lovers !

Sing, mocking bird ! Sing, lark !

Sing, whip-poor-will—your songs in concert ringing ;

Sing in the dewy dawn—sing in the dark ;

But while ye make your sweetest music, hark !

A sweeter song to her my soul is singing !

WEARYIN' FOR YOU.

Jest a-wearyin' fer you—
All the time a-feelin' blue ;
Wishin' fer you—wonderin' when
You'll be comin' home again ;
Restless—don't know *what* to do—
　Jest a-wearyin' fer you !

Keep a-mopin' day by day :
Dull—in everybody's way ;
Folks they smile an' pass along
Wonderin' what on earth is wrong ;
'Twouldn't help 'em if they knew—
　Jest a-wearyin' fer you.

Room's so lonesome, with your chair
Empty by the fireplace there,

Jest can't stand the sight o' it !
Go outdoors an' roam a bit :
But the woods is lonesome, too,
    Jest a-wearyin' fer you.

Comes the wind with sounds that' jes'
Like the rustlin' o' your dress ;
An' the dew on flower an' tree
Tinkles like your steps to me !
Violets, like your eyes so blue—
    Jest a-wearyin' fer you !

Mornin' comes, the birds awake
(Them that sung so fer your sake !),
But there's sadness in the notes
That come thrillin' from their throats !
Seem to feel your absence, too—
    Jest a-wearyin' fer you.

Evenin' comes : I miss you more
When the dark is in the door ;
'Pears jest like *you* orter be
There to open fer me !

Latch goes tinklin'—thrills me through,
Sets me wearyin' fer you !

.   .   .   .   .   .

Jest a-wearyin' fer you—
All the time a-feelin' blue !
Wishin' fer you—wonderin' when
You'll be comin' home again ;
Restless—don't know *what* to do—
Jest a-wearyin' fer you !

A SONG IN GOOD TIME.

Wishin' time,
Fishin' time,
Time to roll over
In shadders
Of medders,
On carpets of clover!

Swingin' time,
Singin' time,
Time to be sippin'
The sunny
Made honey
Of melon juice drippin'!

Merry time,
Berry time,
Time in good meter;
Dove time,
An' love time,
An' life growin' sweeter!

A SONG OF WAITING.

I have waited for your coming as the blossoms
  In the blighted buds of winter wait the spring;
As the robins with the red upon their bosoms
  Await the sweet and loving time to sing.

I have listened for your footstep as the meadows
  Low listen for the dewfall in the night;
As the parched plains droop and dream toward
    the shadows—
  As the leaves in darkness listen for the light!

There is never any rose without the kisses
  Of the spring upon its leaves of red and white;
There is never any meadow if it misses
  The dewfall on its bosom in the night.

There is never any robin's breast that, gleaming,
  Shall feel the thrill and flutter of a wing,

And set the world to loving and to dreaming,
  If there never comes a sunny time to sing.

Let the dew the meadow's violets discover !
  Let the robin sing his sweetest to the close !
There is never any love without a lover—
  You are coming, and the world blooms like a
    rose !

THE OLD PINE BOX.

We didn't care in the long ago
Fer *easy* chairs that was made fer show,
With velvet cushions in red an' black
An' springs that tilted a feller back
'Fore he knowed it—like them in town—
Till his heels went up an' his head went down!
But the seat we loved when we all was poor,
Was the old pine box by the grocery store!

There it stood in the rain an' shine,
Four foot long by the measurin' line;
Under the chiny-berry tree,
Jest as cosy as she could be!
Fust headquarters fer infermation—
Best old box in the whole creation!
Hacked, an' whittled, but feelin' *prime*,
An' so blamed *sociable* all the time!

There we plotted, an' there we'd plan;
Read the news in the paper, an'
Talked o' politics fur an' wide,
An' got mixed up as we argyfied!
An' the old town fiddler sawed away
At "Old Dan Tucker," an' "Nelly Gray,"
An' "Suwannee River," an' fifty more,
On the old pine box by the grocery store.

The boys in the village knowed it well;
It was there they'd come when the meetin' bell
Rung out fer church; fer they knowed the gyrls
Would pass that way in their crimps an' curls,
Smilin' sweeter'n honeycomb
When the boys would ax fer to see 'em home—
Likewise fer the purtiest rose they wore
Past the old pine box by the grocery store!

It heard good music, it got hard knocks,
But still stood faithful—that old pine box!
Fer every feller in town that *could*,
Cut out his name in the willin' wood,

An' his sweetheart's, mixed with the sayin' true
'Bout the rose bein' red an' the violet blue.
Oh, there's boxes still, but there ain't no more
Like the old pine box by the grocery store!

It ain't there now, as it was that day—
Burnt, I reckon, or throwed away ;
An' some o' the folks that the old box knowed
Is fur along on the dusty road ;
An' some's crost over the river wide
An' foun' a home on the other side.
Is they all fergot ? Don't they sigh no more
Fer the old pine box by the grocery store ?

It seems to me, if *my* race was run,
An' I was there, where it's always sun,
With a crown to wear an' a harp to hold—
Loafin' roun' on the streets o' gold,
While the saints was singin' an' sayin' grace
I'd kinder look fer a shady place,
An' dream furever an' *ever*more
Of the old pine box by the grocery store!

THE FIRST KISS.

Sweetheart, 'twas but a while ago—it scarce seems
yesterday,
Though now my locks are white as snow and all
your curls are gray—
When, walking in the twilight haze, ere stars had
smiled above,
I whispered soft: "I love you," and you kissed
me for that love!

The first kiss, dear! and then your hand—your
little hand so sweet,
And whiter than the white, white sand that twin-
kled 'neath your feet—
Laid tenderly within my own! Have queens such
lovely hands?
No wonder that the whip-poor-wills made sweet
the autumn lands!

(52)

It seemed to me that my poor heart would beat to
   death and break,
While all the world, sweetheart! sweetheart!
   seemed singing for your sake;
And every rose that barred the way in glad and
   dying grace,
Forgot its faded summer day and, leaning, kissed
   your face!

I envied all the roses then, and all the rosy ways
That blossomed for your sake are still my life's
   bright yesterdays;
But thinking of that first sweet kiss and that first
   clasp of hands,
Life's whip-poor-wills sing sweeter now through all
   the winter lands!

'POSSUM AN' TATERS.

Talk about *good* eatin', we—
Party jest made up o' three,
An' a woman, sweet, or sweeter
Than " Praise God " in old long meter—
That's the sweetest kind o' song
After sermonts six mile long—
Had a layin' out *that* day,
At the hotel crost the way !
An' I'll say in self-defense,
Never did feel hungry sence !

Talk o' turkey, breast so white,
Goose baked brown an' sarved up right ;
Smokehouse ham an' likes o' that—
Streak o' lean an' streak o' fat ;
Juicy backbone, steak on toas',
Mutton chops 'at some likes mos'—

Sakes! they ain't a 'simmon blossom
To a big, fat, Georgy 'possum!

Had one? Well, you jest kin bet!
('Pears like I kin taste 'im yet!)
Sarved up in old-fashion' style,
'Nough to make a parson smile!
Thar he lay an' graced the feas',
Sides jest gleamin' with the grease,
Brown an' juicy, crisp an' crackin'—
(Sally's lips was jest a-smackin'!)
How they stared—them hotel waiters—
At that 'possum, dressed in taters!

Doctor—fust he made a start,
Carved that 'possum to the heart;
Sich a hurry fer the dressin'
Mos' fergot to ask a blessin'.
"Hol' up, boys," he says: "The case
Is a fittin' one fer grace!"
But the words come sorter jerkin'
When he seen my mouth a-workin'!
(Comes to 'possum—'tain't no cheatin'—
I kin say grace while I'm eatin'!)

Doctor axed a blessin' prime :
" Now, Miss Sally, it's *your* time ! "
Sally went to pass her plate,
But she foun' *mine* couldn't wait !
Warn't no *manners* there *that* day—
Struck her crock'ry jest half way !
Had the biggest kind o' laugh
When my plate come smack in half !
But that didn't stop the game—
'Possum got there jest the same

Every appetite was willin' ;
Taters sweet an' mighty fillin' !
Good old " yams " they raised last year—
Yallerer than Sally's hair !
(I could most eat alligators
Cooked 'longside o' Georgy taters !
When they fix 'em up down South,
Melt like honey in your mouth !
Give a man a right *good* load,
Pay the last red cent he owed !)

Well ! we eat that 'possum ! I
Never seen Time gallop by

As she did at that 'ere feed
With the 'possum in the lead !
Brotherin, this here ain't no fable :
When I drawed off from that table,
Felt that I was goin' to bust
Like the cotton baggin' trust !
But I *didn't*—as you see.
No 'possum gits the best o' *me !*

A BOUQUET.

Red roses, wherefrom the dew drips,
  Staining the turf at my feet,
You were never as red as her lips—
  Or as sweet !

Blue violets, tender and true—
  A mirror for sun-sprinkled skies,
Do you think you were ever as blue
  As her eyes ?

Rare lilies, in garments of white,
  Which winds with warm kisses beguile,
Have you yet known a sunbeam as bright
  As her smile ?

Kiss, lily, rose, violet—kiss !
  Ere time doth your beauty destroy ;
For her white hand hath touched you, and this
  Is your joy !

THE LIGHTNING AGE.

What's the world a-comin' to, a feller'd like to
    know,
When they're makin' ice to order an' manufactur-
    in' snow ?
An' now, as if to vex us, another thing we
    hear :
They're makin' rain in Texas without a word o'
    prayer !

They jest git in a open fiel', where all the folks
    kin view,
An' fire off a cannon ball an' split a cloud in
    two !
An' then you hear a thunderin', and the rain
    comes big and bright ;
But I jest can't help a-wonderin' if that kind o'
    rain is right !

'Pears like the Lord ain't in it, when the string a
 fellow jerks
Kin fire off a cannon 'at'll bust his water-
 works ;
An' it's jest as true as preachin', an' I'm talkin' of
 it plain—
No crop in this here country'll ever grow from
 sich a rain !

The cities—they're gone out o' sight ; it 'pears
 jest like a dream,
Fer when they has a cloudy night they runs the
 stars by steam !
And here's the lightnin' with a song proclaimin'
 man is boss,
An' all the street cars skimmin' 'long without a
 mule or hoss !

An' here's that ringin' telephone, which never
 seems to tire,
But takes your voice a-travellin' crost twenty mile
 o' wire !

They said it reached to t'other worl', an' I reckon
  it was so,
Fer when I axed wher' Molly was, it hollered
  back : *" Hello ! "*

Then, there's that funny phonygraph—I never
  seen the like !
But there's no tellin' nowadays *where* lightnin's
  goin' to strike ;
You jest put in a word or two, an' then take up
  the slack,
An', like a woman when you talk, it keeps a-talkin'
  back !

Lord ! how the world is movin' on, beneath the
  sun an' moon !
I can't help thinkin' I was born a hunder'd year
  too soon ;
But when I go—praise be to God !—it won't be in
  the night,
Fer my grave'll shine like glory in a bright
  electric light !

AT ANDERSONVILLE.

When the weird, wondering wind is still,
There, in the valleys at Andersonville,
At that shivering hour—the grim half way
Of the ghostly march of the dark to-day,
There are sounds too mystical to repeat ;
Eager voices, hurrying feet,
Ribald laughter and jest—and then
The prayers and pleadings of 'prisoned men.

At dead of night, when the wind is still,
There is life in the shadows at Andersonville.
When the hills gloom black in the midnight shade
There are signs of life in the old stockade :
The phantom guards in the prison bounds
Resume their sorrowful, silent rounds ;
While the glowworm's lantern gleams and waves
Adown the aisles of a thousand graves ;

And then to the listening ear there comes
The mystic roll of the muffled drums.

The drama ends and the dreamer wakes :
In the flowering fields and tangled brakes
The birds are singing ; the liquid notes
Rise to heaven from their thrilling throats ;
The sunlight falls with a softened beam
On the voiceless graves where the dead men
    dream ;
While hill and valley and prison sod
Rest in the smile and the peace of God.

But at dead of night, when the wind is still,
There is life in the shadows at Andersonville.

A LAZY CHAP.

I'm the laziest chap, I reckon, that a feller ever
    seen :
Feel drowsy at the tinkle of a bell or tam-
    bourine;
Warn't never made fer reachin' wher' the revenue
    is foun'—
I'm what you'd call "a lazy chap," jest built fer
    lyin' roun'.

Contented ? Mighty right, I am ! when spring
    winds whistle sweet
In the meadows where the daisies make a carpet
    fer your feet.
Where the nestin' birds is chirpin' ; where the
    brook in witchin' play
Goes laughin' on, jest pushin' all the lilies out his
    way,

You'll find me almost any time, a-huntin' shady
    trees,
With the lull song o' the locust, and the drowsy
    drone o' bees
Above me an' all roun' me : I'm a queer one, so
    they say,
Fer I'd ruther hear the birds sing than to shoot
    'em, any day !

I wouldn't nigh be guv'ner, though it's kinder
    great to be,
An' the Georgy legislatur' ain't a drawin' card fer
    me !
An' as fer that old Congress—now, what's *it's* big-
    gest seat
To a feller on a river bank with lilies at his
    feet ?

Jest let 'em *take* the offices an' keep 'em in a
    whirl !
I'd ruther have a vi'let from the sweet hand of a
    girl

Than run the whole United States! So let the
country roll!
Fer a streak o' April sunshine is a-lightin' up my
soul.

I'm a-rollin' in the blossoms as they come a-
tumblin' down,
An' I'm glad as all creation there's a fence 'twixt
me an' town;
I'm rakin' in the sunshine an' takin' of my
ease,
Whistlin' when I want to an' singin' when I
please!

Jest *laziness*, they tell me, an' I reckon that
they're right;
But the world's *so* full o' beauty, an' the sun goes
down at night!
But diff'runt folks has diff'runt minds, an' drink a
diff'runt cup:
When I'm talkin' to the lilies *they're* a-plowin' of
'em up!

My field's a pasture fer the cows, an' though it
    never pays,
It's a powerful source o' pleasure jest to see the
    creeturs graze !
The tinkle, tinkle o' the bells is sich a *pleasin'*
    soun'—
But I'm a lazy chap, you know, jest built fer lyin'
    roun' !

FAITHFUL.

It is something, sweet, when the world goes ill
To know you are faithful and love me still;
To see, when the sunshine has left the skies,
The love-light shining in your dear eyes;
Beautiful eyes, more dear to me
Than all the wealth of the world could be!

It is something, dearest, to feel you near
When life with its sorrows seems hard to bear;
To feel when I falter the clasp divine
Of your tender and trusting hand in mine;
Beautiful hand, more dear to me
Than the tenderest things of earth could be!

Sometimes, dearest, the world goes wrong
For God gives grief with his gift of song,
And poverty, too! But your love is more
To me than riches and golden store;
Beautiful love, until death shall part
It is mine, as you are—my own sweetheart!

"GREEN FIELDS AND RUNNING BROOKS."

Jim Riley sent it to me, as fresh as fresh kin be,
With paper print that's big enough fer any one to
    see;
But sometimes when I'm readin' it the print right
    misty looks—
Jest like as if 'twas rainin' on "Green Fields an'
    Runnin' Brooks!"

But soon the rain—it's over; jest lasts a little
    while,
An' the sun streams on the clover an' makes the
    medders smile;
An' then you smell the violets that peep from cozy
    nooks,
An' hear your sweetheart singin' by "Green Fields
    an' Runnin' Brooks."

(69)

It's good o' Riley jest to think o' me, so fur away;
To take a patch o' winter skies an' weave 'em into
    May ;
To coax the birds to sing fer us, until it kinder
    looks
As if the world was wadin' through "Green Fields
    an' Runnin' Brooks !"

But Jim's "the same old Riley," an' he sings from
    left to right,
Till he sets the world to music an' jest tangles it
    in light ;
An' so, it ain't no wonder that they put him down
    in books,
Like the blessed one he sent me from "Green
    Fields an' Runnin' Brooks !"

A PORTRAIT IN A GRAVE.

Bright in that spot where his brave heart had
   dreamed
   Itself to dust, the faded portrait lay—
   A woman's face that went with him that day
Into the battle where the lightnings gleamed.
Smiling and sweet and beautiful it seemed—
   That face, death-hidden in its frame of clay:
   A soldier of the blue, or of the gray—
Over his dead heart still the dark hair streamed!

Dimly remembered is the conflict done—
   The clamor of the captains—the retreat,
   When Death cried "Halt!" This memory
     above
All others crowns the battle: Here was one
   Whose dying lips a woman's kiss made sweet—
   Whose grave is glorious with a woman's love!

THROUGH THE WHEAT.

When she came tripping through the wheat
It seemed to bend to kiss her feet,
And roses all the sod made sweet
    And birds sang cheery;

The honey bees were humming low—
Gold specks on roses white as snow,
Sweet roses—not so sweet, I know,
    As she was—Mary!

Her footstep seemed to wake a sound
Of tinkling music from the ground
That thrilled the winds that whistled round
    With sweet caresses;

And on her forehead, white and sleek,
The rarest blossoms fell to wreak
Their love, and played at hide-and-seek
    In her gold tresses.

Down fell the scythe upon the grass,
And " Mary, Mary, will you pass?"
"You're in my way," she said.   "Alas!
  I must be going!"

"Not till you pay the forfeit sweet
Of coming this way through the wheat;
Ah! Mary—lips were made to meet—
  A kiss you're owing!"

Up went the dainty finger tips,
To shield the rich and rosy lips,
And all their red was in eclipse—
  My luck seemed missing.

A moment only!   Then, as she
Fled like a shaft of light from me,
She cried: "I paid no forfeit—see?
  You did the kissing!"

THE TRUANT.

Oh, school's took in, but it ain't took *me*,
   Fer I'm goin' 'crost the meadows jest a-skim-
   min'!
When I ain't kite-flyin' wher' the wind blows free,
I'm six yards furder 'an my folks kin see,
   Fishin', or strippin' off fer swimmin'!

Oh, school's took in, but it ain't took *me*,
   Fer the pond with the tadpoles is a-brimmin'!
When I ain't in the top o' the chinyberry tree,
I'm six yards furder 'an my folks kin see,
   Fishin', or strippin' off fer swimmin'!

A LITTLE BIT OF A BOY.

There was never a smile in a weary while,
  And never a gleam of joy,
Till his eyes of light made the whole world
    bright—
  A little bit of a boy !

He came one day when the world was May,
  And thrilling with life and joy ;
And with all the roses he seemed to play—
  A little bit of a boy !

But he played his part with a human heart,
  And time can never destroy
The memory sweet of the pattering feet
  Of that little bit of a boy !

We had wondered how he could play all day
  With never a dream of rest ;

But once he crept in the dark and slept
 Still on his mother's breast !

.   .   .   .   .   .

There was never a smile in a weary while,
 And never a gleam of joy ;
But the world seems dim since we dreamed of
  him—
 A little bit of a boy !

JENNY AND I.

Jenny and I were lovers,
  Many and many a year ;
Poor as I be—but Jenny gave me
  The gold of her moonlight hair ;
And I said, " Too ragged a lover
  To wed with the winsome witch ! "
But she bent her head, with her lips o' red,
  And kissed me, and made me rich !

Jenny and I were lovers,
  Yonder—in storm and fair ;
But her blue-bright eyes made the summer skies,
  And her smile the spring o' the year.
Poor as a wayside beggar,
  With her tresses around me curled,
Like veins o' gold in the rugged mold,
  I was richer than all the world !

Jenny and I were lovers,
  With only the sky above ;
And we cared not for a painted cot,
  For heaven was over our love.
The brooks were our mirrors—the water wine
  That sparkled by hill and glen ;
Her face beamed pink where I stooped to drink,
  And the water was sweeter then !

Jenny and I were lovers,
  Many and many a year ;
But the rose was wed to her lips o' red,
  And the moonlight envied her hair ;
And the red rose creeps where her true heart
    sleeps,
  And the moonlight falleth drear
Where Jenny and I were lovers—
  Many and many a year !

THE FAMILY RECORD.

Thar's John—he is a doctor, an' William kinder
    laws,
An' Reuben, he's a traveler in the missionary
    cause ;
An' Moses runs a grocery store, an' Zekiel, he's
    the mayor ;
An' Bob, he deals in real estate, where all the cash
    is clear ;
An' Jim, he's tradin' horses, an' Ben, he runs the
    mill,
An' Jeremiah deals in corn an' moonlight at the
    still ;
An' Jackson—well, he ain't no 'count—jes' keeps
    'em on the stir
To make a livin' fer him : Jack's a *politicianer !*

SINGING OF YOU.

Blossoms and blossoms and blossoms! and birds
    singing of 'em, so sweet!
Pressing the down of their bosoms 'gainst the
    flowers that fall at your feet!
Clinging and swinging and flinging their souls to
    the heavens so blue—
Oh, sweet to my soul is their singing, because they
    are singing of you!

    Singing of you
    In the dawn and the dew—
Singing of heaven and singing of you!

Blossoms and blossoms and blossoms! sparkling
    with beautiful pearls,
Twining themselves for your tresses, and falling
    and kissing your curls!

And all the birds swinging and flinging their souls
    to God's heavens of blue,
And my soul dreaming soft in their singing, be-
    cause they are singing of you!

    Singing of you
    In the dawn and the dew—
    Singing of heaven and singing of you!

LITTLE ELAINE.

Where have you gone, little Elaine,
With the eyes like violets wet with rain—
Silvery April rain, that throws
Melting diamonds over the rose?
(Ah, never were eyes as bright as those!)
You have left me alone; but where have you
    flown?
God knows, my dear, God knows!

Where have you gone, little Elaine,
With laughing lips of the crimson stain—
Lips that smiled as the sunlight glows
When morning breaks like a white, sweet rose
Over the wearisome winter snows?
Shall I miss their song my whole life long?
God knows, my dear, God knows!

You have left me lonely, little Elaine :
I call to you, but I call in vain ;
I sing to you when the twilight throws
Its dying light on my life's last rose,
While the tide of Memory ebbs and flows.
Is it God's own will I should miss you still ?
God knows, my dear, God knows !

OUT OF THE RACE.

Let 'em fix their slates fer votin'—
Let 'em fight to git the place;
While they're jawin' I'm a co'tin'—
Smackin' of a purty face!
I ain't with 'em—take my note in—
Tell 'em that I'm out the race!

Let 'em tell their jokes so funny,
(They ain't never understood!)
While the bees is storin' honey
In my hives of hollowed wood;
While I'm makin' heaps of money
Fishin' fer the neighborhood!

THE PARTING OF POOR JACK.

'A made a finer end, and went away, an it had been any Christom child ; . . . for after I saw him fumble with the sheets, and play with flowers, . . . I knew there was but one way. . . . So 'a bade me lay more clothes on his feet . . . and all was as cold as any stone.—MRS. QUICKLY.

I do forgive him for his raid
On Gad's Hill—valiant knight!
For Mistress Quickly's scores unpaid—
The sword he hacked for fight;
For all his frequent calls for sack—
(The brawler bluff and old!)
Because of that sad day—poor Jack!—
That day he was a-cold!

That day when, stealing to his den,
(As history repeats)
He "babbled of green fields," and then
Pale, "fumbled with the sheets";

Crept to his darkened lodge—alack!
   Sir John, so stout and bold:
" The king had killed his heart "—poor Jack!—
   That day he was a-cold!

And Mistress Quickly I revere
   In that she stood his cause
And faced them down that Jack was there
   Where " Arthur's bosom " was!
Forgot were all his unpaid scores—
   Her grievous wrongs untold;
She had not turned him out o' doors
   That day he was a-cold!

Poor Jack! he did not hearken then
   To "chimes o' midnight " wild;
But parted from his fellow-men
   " Like any Christom child."
His cloudy memory bore him back
   To flowery days of old;
He "babbled of green fields "—poor Jack!—
   That day he was a-cold!

So, I forgive him for his raid
  On Gad's Hill—with the rest;
For Shallow's thousand pounds unpaid,
  And every brawling jest;
For Bardolph's nose, a-shine with sack,
  And Pistol's tirades bold;
He parted from us young—poor Jack!—
  That day he was a-cold!

A DAY OFF.

When a feller takes a day off—sets his soul to
    loafin, roun'
Where the hills climb up to heaven an' the rushin'
    rivers soun',
'Pears like the world is newer, with a good deal
    more o' light,
An' his eyes is seein' truer, an' his heart is beatin'
    right!

When a feller takes a day off, there is lots o' things
    to see;
I can hear the winds away off, jest a welcomin' o'
    me;
An' the violets peep so purty! an' the rose I use-
    ter miss
Feels the red a-rushin' roun' it, an' comes climbin'
    fer a kiss!

When a feller takes a day off—oh, he learns a lot
    o' things
From the very doves a-flyin', with the music in
    their wings;
From the hills an' from the valleys, where the
    dreams an' dews is foun'—
When a feller takes a day off, an' his soul is loafin'
    roun'!

AFTER.

After the noonday heat,
Cool shadows, soft descending from above,
   And all the bells of twilight chiming sweet,
And love—thy love!

After the storm and strife,
Over the calm seas, swift and sure—the dove,
   Bearing the olive through a rainbowed life,
Sweet with thy love!

After the darkened light,
Faith that finds wings, stars and great stars above,
   And earth's last memory sweet with thy "Good-
      night"—
Thy lips, thy love!

'TWAS FAR AWAY.

'Twas far away where skies are fair,
  And sweet with song and light,
When I had but my scythe, my dear,
  And you your needles bright.

So far away! And yet, to-day,
  For all the distance drear,
My heart keeps chime with that dear time
  And dreams the old dreams there!

There, where love learned its sweetest words
  And built its brightest bowers;
Where sang the rarest mocking birds
  And bloomed the fairest flowers!

And fields were golden-rich, and clear
  The streams flowed in the light—
When I had but my scythe, my dear,
  And you your needles bright!

(oi)

How soft and sweet across the wheat
 Your dear voice seemed to roam,
When stars of love peeped pale above
 And I went dreaming home!

Life had no sweeter joy than this—
 To rest a little while
There, where you met me with a kiss
 And blest me with a smile!

So far that sweet time seems to-day,
 Here 'neath these darkened skies;
And yet, across the weary way
 You light me with your eyes!

And I would give earth's gold to share
 Once more that day—that night,
When I had but my scythe, my dear,
 And you your needles bright.

WATERMELON SONG.

Oh, the Georgia watermelon—it's a-growin' cool
    an' green,
An'll soon be pullin' heavy at the stem;
An' the knife—it needs a whettin', an' the blade is
    gittin' keen.
  Oh, the Georgia watermelon is a gem!

      Melons cool an' green—
      Jest the best you ever seen!
      See the sweet juice drippin'
      From them melons cool an' green!

Oh, the Georgia watermelon—with the purtiest
    sort o' stripe!
It ain't a streak o' fat an' streak o' lean;
You thump her with your fingers, an' you hear her
    answer, "*Ripe !*"
  Oh, the Georgia watermelon cool an' green!

Melons cool an' green—
Jest the best you ever seen !
See the sweet juice drippin'
From them melons cool an' green !

When you pull a Georgia melon you must know
   what you are at,
An' look out how your knife is goin' in ;
Put one half on *this* side o' you, the other half on
   that,
An' then you git between 'em an' begin !

Melons cool an' green—
They're the best you ever seen !
How the juice comes drippin'
From them melons cool an' green !

They're mighty, *mighty* fillin' with their flamin'
   hearts o' red—
Like the reddest o' the roses in the South ;
When cotton's down to nothin', take the place o'
   meat an' bread ;
Make you think a hive o' honey's in your
   mouth !

Melons cool an' green—
Best the country ever seen!
Oh, the meltin' sweetness
Of them melons cool an' green!

But it's 'way ahead o' honey—as a slice or two
  will prove;
It's slicker, an' it's *sweeter* as it slips!
There ain't no "nigger problem" when the melon's
  on the move—
Make the white man an' the nigger smack his
  lips!

Melons cool an' green—
Don't want *any* fence between!
But I'd outclimb all creation
For them melons cool an' green!

THE DUEL.

There, in the merciless morn's first glow,
Grim, defiant, I faced my foe ;

He who had wronged me with savage hate,
Face to face on the field of fate.

And I said, " He must die ; he has played his part ;
My sword shall cleave through his hateful heart ! "

Then to the battle : with one true thrust
He stood defenseless, his sword in dust.

I marked the spot where his false heart lay,
I lifted my glittering blade to slay ;

When lo ! in my fury I seemed to feel
A hand that clutched at the lifted steel :

A hand that warded the blow I dealt ;
And wild before me a woman knelt !

I could not strike him—my hated foe;
In wrath and mercy I bade him go.

Fool! forgetting the wrongs of years,
To drown revenge in a woman's tears!

FOR SALLY.

It's happy every mornin',
   Every evenin' I will be;
Fer I hoe the corn fer Sally,
   An' she bakes the bread fer me.

It's a little farm I'm runnin',
   An' the soil is kinder rough;
But I'm workin' it fer Sally,
   An' the crop grows fast enough.

All day long I hear her singin',
   An' a lot of joy it brings;
Fer there ain't no song that's sweeter
   Than the song that Sally sings.

Fer she sings because she's happy,
   An' I stop the plow an' hoe
When I hear her, feelin' thankful
   That it's me has made her so!

She keeps the pails all shinin',
  An' the bees a-workin' hard ;
Calls the cows up fer the milkin',
  Trains the roses in the yard ;

An' she keeps furever singin'
  When the household troubles press ;
With a kiss fer little fingers
  Always tuggin' at her dress.

Oh, it's happy every mornin',
  Every evenin' I will be ;
Fer I hoe the corn fer Sally,
  An' she bakes the bread fer me !

ONE SAD DAY.

One sad day when the sun's gold crown
  Jeweled the desolate, dreamy west,
I came with a burden, and laid it down
  Under the lilies and leaves to rest ;
And, weeping, I left it and went my way
  With the Twilight whispering, " God knows
    best ! "

One sad day—it was long ago,
  And thorny the paths my feet have pressed
Since with tears and kisses I laid it low—
  Soul of my soul and life of my breast !
But kneeling now in the dark to pray,
  There comes with a song from the sunless west
The same sweet voice that I heard that day—
  The Twilight whispering, " God knows best ! "

THE OLD POSTMASTER.

Been runnin' of the office
  Fer fifteen year an' more ;
Beat all the other candidates—
  Walked in an' locked the door !

He wears two pair o' spectacles,
  His sight is growin' dim ;
He knows each man that ever
  Had a letter writ to him.

He says : " Bill Brown, here's somethin'—
  Handwritin's kinder slant ;
I guess it's from your daddy,
  Or a letter from your aunt ! "

He strikes a yaller envelope
  With printin' on one end ;
He han's it to the groceryman :
  "About them goods, my friend ! "

Knows everybody's business,
　An' tells 'em of it, too ;
" A letter from your sweetheart,"
　Or " Another bill fer you!"

No politics kin hurt him,
　No matter who may win ;
He sees the presidents go out
　While he keeps stayin' in.

But the truth about the matter
　To all is mighty clear :
He's been a-runnin' things so long,
　They've done fergot he's there!

A FAIR POLITICIAN.

She has asked, " How will you vote?"
And I make no vague condition
In reply, because I note :
Dora is a politician !
Would her red-rose lips condemn
If I voted straight for them ?

How the gold curls gleam above,
How the blue eyes beam beneath !
There's no politics in love—
Just a kiss, a rose, a wreath !
When her curls and eyes I note,
Need she ask me how I'll vote ?

But the question still she plies
With the shyest, sweetest art,
And the twinkle in her eyes
Makes a light around my heart !
And I answer, bending o'er her,
" By God's grace I'll vote for Dora ! "

A COUNTRY PHILOSOPHER.

The cold has killed the corn off an' blighted all
    the wheat;
The ice is on the peach blooms an' the apple blos-
    soms sweet,
An' the country is in mournin' from the mountains
    to the sea,
But the good Lord runs the weather, an' it ain't
    a-botherin' me !

The bees was out fer honey an' a-workin' fer their
    lives,
But the blizzard stopped their buzzin', an' they're
    froze up in their hives ;
An' there won't be any sweet'nin' fer the coffee or
    the tea,
But the good Lord runs the weather, an' it ain't
    a-botherin' me !

The mockin' birds was singin' jest the sweetest
    kind o' notes,
But now they're sittin' silent with a flannel roun'
    their throats ;
An' there won't be any music 'til the summer
    time to be,
But the good Lord runs the weather, an' it ain't
    a-botherin' me !

It don't make any difference *what* these changin'
    seasons bring ;
If it's cold, the fire's a-blazin', an' I hear the chim-
    ney sing ;
If it's hot, the trees is shady, with the breeze
    a-blowin' free,
Fer the good Lord runs the weather, an' it ain't
    a-botherin' me !

THE SHIPS OF MELTON.

How sail the ships to Melton,
  That lieth far and fair
And dreamlike in the haven
  Where skies are calm and clear ?
With blown sails leaning whitely,
  Sure winged 'neath storm or star,
They straightly steer—for still they hear
  The love-bells o'er the bar.

How sail the ships to Melton,
  Within whose cots of white
Love dreams of love and listens
  For footsteps in the night ?
Like gulls, their glad way winging,
  They speed from lands afar ;
For still they hear in music clear
  The love-bells o'er the bar.

How sail the ships to Melton ?
  Love-blown across the foam ;
For still the sea sings ever
  The songs of love and home ;
Nor spicy isles with splendid smiles
  Can win their sails afar,
While softly swells that chime of bells—
  The love-bells o'er the bar.

Oh, ships that sail to Melton,
  With captains glad and grand,
The stars that light the ocean
  Are the stars that light the land ;
But say for me, adrift at sea
  On lonely wrecks afar :
My heart still hears, and dreaming nears
  The love-bells o'er the bar !

THEY'VE HUNG BILL JONES.

They've hung Bill Jones to the sycamore tree,
  An' his wife an' his mother is a-weepin';
An' his children's come from the house to see,
  An' the col' wind a-wailin' an' a-creepin'!

Oh, the col' wind's a-wailin' an' a-creepin',
An' the wife an' the mother is a-weepin';
    An' the children's there
    Fer to stand an' stare,
An' the col' wind a-wailin' an' a-creepin'!

They've hung Bill Jones fer a crime of his,
  An' his wife an' his mother is a-dyin';
An' his children's took where the orphants is—
  An' the col' wind a-creepin' an' a-sighin'!

Oh, the col' wind's a-creepin' an' a-sighin',
An' the wife an' the mother is a-dyin';
    An' his children's 'way
    Where the orphants stay—
An' the col' wind a-creepin' an' a-sighin'!

THE TOP FLOOR.

Noisy sparrows build their nests
　Underneath the eaves :
I can almost touch their breasts
　In the straw and leaves.
From the housetops o'er the 'way
　Curious pigeons peer
At me as I rhyme each day—
　Only tenant here.

How they pout, and coo and kiss
　All the bright day long !
I can learn a trick from this :
　Love—and then a song !
Song for sixpence !　It is well;
　For the music floats
Freely as the notes that swell
　From the birds' clear throats.

Here's a song, then : Life is sweet,
  Though it hurries by ·
Cheerily the world I greet,
  Up six stories high.
Knowing little of its cares ;
  Closer to the skies ;
Love—who will not climb the stairs—
In the window flies.

And I hold a man may love
  Nobly, truly, when
He is lodged so far above
  All his fellow-men !
For he breathes a purer air :
  Days are never dim :
Stars that tinge the atmosphere
  Brighter seem to him.

Suns are warmer—or, at least,
  Shine with greater grace ;
Nature is his soul's high priest,
  And his temple—space !

And the world's rude voices rise
  Murmuringly aloft ;
For the distance to the skies
  Melts and makes them soft.

In a garret life must be
  Far from busy throngs ;
Little sparrows, chirp to me :
  Teach my soul your songs !
Teach me that God's world is sweet,
  Though I dwell above ;
With the print of children's feet
  In the paths of love.

Sing, and build your little nests
  Underneath the eaves ;
Though the heart that loves you rests
  With life's fallen leaves.
Sing ! for life is kind and sweet
  As it hurries by :
Cheerily the world we greet,
  Up six stories high !

DON'T YOU?

When you see the hills away off
  Lookin' green an' gold an' blue,
It is time to take a day off
  With the daisies an' the dew.

  Don't you wish
  Fer a fish
Where the trees is goin' " swish " ?
When you hear the birds a-singin',
An' the cattle bells a-ringin',
An' the honeysuckles swingin'—
Don't you wish ?

When March is headin' May off,
  With a rumple in his curls,
It is time to take a day off,
  Huntin' violets with the girls.

Don't you pine
Fer the shine
Of the meadows fair and fine?
Fer the lilied rills a-flowin',
Fer the woods with blossoms blowin',
Fer the world with beauty glowin'—
Don't you pine?

MY LADY.

In my poor cot there dwelleth not
  A lady lulled in laces
And satins fine ; none such is mine—
  But very sweet her face is :
For God, when first her heart did beat,
Smiled on her face and made it sweet.

She robeth not her dear self in
  Rare gowns of queenly splendor ;
She hath won all that she would win—
  A heart's love, loyal, tender ;
She is not rich ; and yet I know
One smile of love can make her so !

No jewels glitter on her hands,
  And ne'er to love betrayed her ;
Of all the ladies of the lands,
  She's just as God hath made her ;

For when he made the morning he
Made one rose for himself and me!

And close beside my heart I wear
  That flower that fadeth never;
And if I pray, 'tis but this prayer :
  To keep that rose forever.
But lo! my lady comes, and she
Brings roses of her love to me!

THE RATTLESNAKE.

I'm the first of the season ; my venomous head
Is poised for the conflict :   Beware how you
    tread !
My fangs, they are fatal—my warning expressed :
You just touch the button, and I'll do the rest !

Yet, far from these liars of men I repose,
And coiled in contentment I lazily doze,
Till their footsteps arouse me from visions un-
    blest ;
Then, they touch the button, and I do the rest !

What liars they are—all these creatures called
    men ;
They multiply each of my rattles by ten ;
And hence, with my black tongue my wrath is ex-
    pressed,
And they touch the button, and I do the rest !

A LITTLE WAY.

A little way to walk with you, my own—
　　Only a little way,
Then one of us must weep and walk alone
　　Until God's day.

A little way !　It is so sweet to live
　　Together, that I know
Life would not have one withered rose to give
　　If one of us should go.

And if these lips should ever learn to smile,
　　With thy heart far from mine,
'Twould be for joy that in a little while
　　They would be kissed by thine !

DIDN'T THINK OF LOSIN' HIM.

Always wuz abusin' him—
Rough an' rougher usin' him,
Love an' all refusin' him,
  Though his tears 'ud fall ;
Didn't think o' losin' him—
  Not at all !

He, poor feller, he'd jest sigh,
With a waterin' o' the eye—
Say : " It's all my fault," and try
  T' stave 'em off a while !
" *Some day I'll lay down an' die—*
  Then they'll smile."

An' he did.   God's sometimes heap
Kinder to His poor, lost sheep
Than the ones 'at has their keep ;
  So, one lonesome day,

He jest told him, "*Go to sleep*,"
    In His own kind way.

Then the poor, sad, weary eyes
Smiled their thanks to God's own skies,
With a kind o' sweet surprise—
    And the heart growed still.
Said one of 'em : " Thar he lies;
    It's God's will ! "

.   .   .   .   .   .

Always wuz abusin' him—
Rough an' rougher usin' him,
Love an' all refusin' him,
    Though his tears 'ud fall ;
Didn't think o' losin' him—
    Not at all !

THE HOME KEEPER.

About her household moving glad each day,
  With heartful care of all the simplest things ;
  And near her side a child voice coos and sings—
She hears the noise of pattering feet at play,
And pauses oft to kiss the lips that say
  "Mother!" and joys to feel the hand that
    clings
  Close to her heart, as to her apron strings—
Nor would she chide that little hand away !

Then, when the day hath drifted to the dark,
  And brightening stars loom through the twilight
    late,
  She feels the heart within her bosom stir
At every leaf that strikes the lattice. . . . Hark !
  Her life's reward—a footstep at the gate,
  And love that comes to claim the love of her !

JUNE DREAMS.

There's something in the hazy, lazy, daisy atmosphere
That makes a fellow mellow all the soul he has to
  spare
In the scented, sweet, contented subtle season
  when the tunes,
Of a million birds make music for a million, trillion Junes!

You are dreaming in the gleaming—you are blind-
  ed by the glow
Of the white light and the bright light, where the
  splendid rivers flow;
Or in dells where bells of twilight ring their re-
  quiem of rest,
You are drifting with the rose leaves to the
  Night's voluptuous breast!

Life is languor, with no anger of a storm to strike
and slay
The peace that makes the perfect and splendid-
vista'd day ;
Life is glory, and the story, told in Love's melodious tunes
Makes the world move to the music of a million,
trillion Junes !

A SONG OF LIFE.

He that clingeth unto life
For the fond lips of a wife
Hath, I know, great joy to live:
Earth hath nothing more to give—
Of all gifts the heavens confer,
Sweeter than the love of her!

He that is to life beguiled
By the clinging of a child
Hath, I know, great store of grace,
And with Love a dwelling place;
For all heaven hath dreamed and smiled
In the sweet face of a child.

He that unto life is drawn
When the dark hath drowned the dawn;
When no wife's lips sigh or sing,
When no child's arms clasp and cling,

Still hath hope—for in the night
Cometh dreams and gleams of light!

So, though love be lost to thee
Life, though lonely, sweet may be ;
Canst thou take, when sore opprest,
Others' burdens to thy breast,
Love unto the loveless give ?
Thou shalt bless thyself and live!

A SHARP POLITICIAN.

Jim Jones—he run fer Congress; they beat him
    out o' that—
Likewise a mule, a pair o' boots, an' bran new
    beaver hat;
But when he saw that he was whipped—did Jones
    feel sad an' sick?
Not him! He bought another mule an' run fer
    Sheriff quick!

Then they put up another man, they said was
    shore to win,
An' shore enough Jim Jones went out while that
    same chap went in!
But did they find him sulkin' when he knowed
    they'd whipped him clear?
Not him! He bought another mule an' run like
    bricks fer mayor!

An' then he got elected, an' when he held the fort
He summoned them as whipped him out to come
　　into his court;
An' he fined 'em each ten dollars—it was all jest
　　like a dream—
An' when they paid an' went away Jim Jones was
　　rich as cream!

BLACKBERRIES.

Blackberries—do you know
  Where to find them ?
Oh, their briers prick you so—
  Never mind them !

Get your cap, you queen in curls!
  (Don't be shy, dear !)
For the sun will kiss the girls.
  (So will I, dear !)

'Tis a quaint cap that you take—
  Nay, a bonnet ;
But the sunbeams—they will make
  Ribbons on it !

Let me tie the strings.   (I'll hold
  My caresses.)
Now it's hidden half the gold
  Of your tresses !

But we go where drops of dew
  (Looking-glasses)
Paint the rosy face of you
  On the grasses.

O'er the bars I climb, and so—
  In the clover,
(I have willing arms, you know!)
  Take you over.

Now the birds sing in the blooms
  Where they've found us,
Where a million sweet perfumes
  Swoon around us:

" Berries, berries, black and sweet,
  Love, forsake them!
They were made for birds to eat—
  Do not take them!

" In the hedges, by the rills—
  In shy covers,
They are sweetening our bills
  For our lovers."

But the berries black we pull
(Play your part, love!)
Till your bonnet's brimming full—
Like my heart, love!

Now you've spilled them! Let them go,
While love sips, dear,
Sweeter juices than they know
From your lips, dear.

Give the berries to the birds,
Singing near them;
Love would say some little words:
Will you hear them?

Suns may set, or suns may shine,
Birds sing never:
Love is thine and love is mine,
Sweet, forever!

STILL IN THE RING.

TO C. J. B.

You say I've stopped from singin', and some sor-
　　row you've expressed,
That my muse is gittin' lazy since I left the sweet
　　Southwest ;
Well, maybe so an' *not* so : we're better when we're
　　brief :
But the rose of song's a-bloomin', though the frost
　　is on the leaf.

I'll tell you why I'm quiet—why I don't chirp as
　　before :
'Tain't because my whistle's broken an' needs
　　fixin' at the store ;
But I'm somethin' of a stranger to these towerin'
　　hills of snow,
An' my songs—they're all behind me, where the
　　Southland roses grow.

(130)

I'm always thinkin', thinkin' of the times that used
    to be,
Where the springs and golden autumns flushed the
    friendly fields of Lee ;
An' as I look back yonder, on them fur-off plains
    an' skies,
The sun may be a-shinin', but—*it's rainin' roun' my*
    eyes !

Well ! here's a greetin' to you : I'm still inside the
    ring,
An' a-lovin' an' a-list'nin' to the songs the others
    sing ;
But my harp, jest fer the present, is reposin' on
    the shelf,
An' my heart makes all the music, but it keeps it
    to itself !

A DAY IN THE WOODS.

A mocking bird sweet singing on a spray
  Of dewy blossoms, lightly shaken down;
  A river running by the rushes brown,
Its green banks drifting dreamily away,
And the sun centered in the splendid day!
  Far off, faint echoes of a noisy town,
  And hills that wear a blue and golden crown,
And fields of corn, and meadows sweet with May!

And then—the bells of twilight—restful, sweet!
  A lulling murmur from the languid rills—
    A gray star glimmering in the blended blue;
And my heart heaving with a happier beat,
  Answering the calling of the whip-poor-wills
    That time my footsteps home to love and
      you!

JIM TUCK'S OLD WOMAN.

Jim Tuck's old woman's a sight, I say,
  Whenever she takes a turn :
She don't stand none o' your foolish play,
  An' none o' your tricks in her'n.
I found that out 'fore election day,
  'Thout any remarks from him ;
When she said in a quiet an' meanin' way :
  " I reckon you'll vote fer Jim ? "

Now, you know, Jim Tuck an' myself wuz dead
  Sot 'gin one ernuther—cross ez
Two sticks, an' couldn't be drove ner led,
  An' never could set hosses ;
So, when she made that remark I said :
  " His chances with me is slim."
"Oh, no !" she cried—an' she looked cross-eyed:
  " I reckon you'll vote fer Jim ! "

That riled me, an' so—'fore I seemed to know,
    I blazed rite out an' cussed
Jim outen the county—high an' low—
    But brotherin', she never fussed ;
Jest moved a step when I turned to go—
    That woman wuz fur from slim—
An' locked the door an' remarked once more :
    " I reckon you'll vote fer Jim ! "

An' sayin' this, with a sudden sweep
    She riz with the kitchen broom ;
An' fallin' foul o' me, in a heap,
    She walloped me roun' the room !
She fit an' fout, an' she jumped erbout
    Ten foot—an' she wuzn't slim—
An' still she'd shout as she laid me out :
    " I reckon you'll vote fer Jim ! "

'Twas gittin' lively fer both of us,
    An' so, I begin debatin'
That mebbe Jim wuzn't as big a cuss
    As the feller that I'd been hatin' ;

An' so—but all o' you fellers know
The story 'bout her an' him:
He's sheriff now, an'—I can't tell how,
But I reckon I voted fer Jim!

THE SHOWER.

Fall, gentle rain, in blessed, brimming drops;
  Cool with thy kiss the city's burning streets;
  Moisten the meadows where the hot sun beats,
And fall refreshing on the thirsty crops;
The warm wind for thy cordial greeting stops;
  The panting flock a merry welcome bleats;
  The famished fields unfold a thousand sweets;
The grass bends dimpling on the mountain tops!

Fall, gentle rain, on the rejoicing land!
  The incense rises from the dusty plain;
    The valley's violets, for a moment blurred,
Twinkle for joy! and where the live oaks stand,
  There rings a glad thanksgiving for the rain
    In the wild music of the mocking bird!

(136)

APRIL.

Fellers, this is April—know it by the breeze
Caperin' roun' an' rumplin' the ringlets o' the
trees ;
Know it by my wishin' fer the woods an' streams ;
All day long I'm fishin'—ketch 'em in my dreams !

Fellers, this is April—sunny, soft an' sweet ;
April from her bright eyes to the roses roun' her
feet !
Like a country maiden, rosy-faced she trips,
Sunshine on her yellow curls an' honey on her
lips !

Fellers, this is April : git out in the air !
Let her run her fingers fer a minute through your
hair !
Hear her birds a-singin', while the world so blest
To her lips is clingin', an' dreamin' on her breast !

Fellers, this is April, with a lap o' pearls;
Seems to me you'd know it, holdin' han's with all
    the gyrls,
An' huntin' wild flowers with 'em! Oh, May is
    sweet to see,
But April with her violets is joy enough fer me!

UNCLE JIM.

Uncle Jim—he only saw
  The ocean once, and then
They put him in a bathing suit,
  Just like the other men ;
But when, a-tiptoe on the beach,
  He saw the billows rise,
And, breaking o'er him, strive to reach
  To mansions in the skies,
He jerked that bathing suit of red
  ('Twas well the sun had set !)
And cried, as fast the bathers fled :
  " This blamed thing's ringin' wet !"

A LITTLE BOY FOR SALE.

Here is a little boy—
A little boy for sale !
With all of his dimpled cheeks of joy
And the voice of a nightingale ;—
A little boy for sale,
A boy that is fair and fat ;
If you missed the joy of that little boy,
Would you know where your heart was at ?

Here is a little boy—
A little boy for sale !
Will you buy him now ? Here's a curly brow
And the voice of a nightingale !
A little boy for sale—
Ho ! buyers, from east and west !
It shall not fail that this nightingale
Shall sing near the mother nest !

Some birds there be that fly
From the land o'er the ocean's foam,
But the voice of this bird is always heard
Where the sweet birds sing at home!
At home where the light is bright—
At home where the love is best!
Oh, the nightingale! and the boy for sale!
They are bought for the mother's breast!

A FISHERMAN IN TOWN.

I jest set here a-dreamin'—
    A-dreamin' every day,
Of the sunshine that's a-gleamin'
    On the rivers—fur away ;

An' I kinder fall to wishin'
    I was where the waters swish ;
Fer if the Lord made fishin',
    Why—a feller orter fish !

While I'm studyin', or a-writin',
    In the dusty, rusty town,
I kin feel the fish a-bitin'—
    See the cork a-goin' down !

An' the sunshine seems a-tanglin'
    Of the shadows, cool an' sweet ;
With the honeysuckles danglin',
    An' the lilies at my feet !

So, I nod, an' fall to wishin'
  I was where the waters swish;
Fer if the Lord made fishin',
  Why—a feller orter fish!

THE OLD SCHOOL EXHIBITIONS.

Oh, the old school exhibitions ! will they ever come
    again,
With the good, old-fashioned speaking from the
    girls and boys so plain ?
Will we ever hear old " Iser," with its rapid roll
    and sweep,
And " Pilot, 'tis a fearful night ; there's danger on
    the deep " ?

Sweet Mary doesn't raise her lambs like Mary did
    of old ;
Their fleece is not " as white as snow "; they're
    wandering from the fold ;
The boy upon " the burning deck " is not one half
    as fine—
He was not " born at Bingen, at Bingen on the
    Rhine ! "

The girls don't speak in calico, the boys in cotton
jeans;
They've changed the old-time dresses 'long with
the old-time scenes;
They smile and speak in crooked Greek; in broad‑
cloth and in lace;
And you can't half see the speaker for the collar
'round the face!

Oh, the old school exhibitions! They are gone forever more!
The old schoolhouse is deserted, and the grass has
choked the door;
And the wind sweeps 'round the gables, with a low
and mournful whine
For the old boys "born at Bingen—at Bingen on
the Rhine!"

IN ABSENCE.

Your mocking birds are mute
  Amid the peach blooms and the pines that sigh-
    ing
Delay the winds that pass them like a lute
  Whose sweetest notes are dying.

Your lilies bend and weep,
  Because in vain they lift their lips to kiss
    you ;
The morning-glories 'round your casement creep,
  And, looking in, they miss you.

Your haunted brook glides o'er
  The sparkling stones where wild flowers lean to
    win it,
And moans its way, because it feels no more
  Your face reflected in it.

Birds, winds, brooks, flowers—they keep
　Sad vigils where the lonely light is streaming;
And I—across the darkness and the deep
　My soul drifts to you, dreaming!

IN THE FIELDS.

Oh, maiden under the skies so blue,
  Of the eyes and tresses brown,
I'd rather be walking the fields with you
  Than going my way to the town !
Is it far to your dwelling ?   But here's a rose ;
Perhaps you slipped from its heart—who knows ?

It is like your face ; it is like the smile
  Of your lips so red and sweet.
Do the roses bloom for a little while
  And their hearts then cease to beat ?
How fair were the roses my youth-time knew !
Were I a rose I would bloom for you.

Do you roam through the summers sweet and long
  Over these fields so fair,
And blend your voice with the harvest song
  That thrills through the scented air ?

When you bind the wheat with a golden skein
Are the tares not mixed with the ripened grain?

Sowing and reaping my life has known,
  And now with the gathered sheaves
There are fruitless weeds that have heedless
  grown,
  And thorns 'neath the rose's leaves.
Sowing and reaping, the harvest seems
Less than my labor and less than my dreams.

.   .   .   .   .   .

Oh, maiden under the skies so blue,
  Of the eyes and tresses brown,
I'd rather be walking the fields with you
  Than going my way to the town!
Is it far to your dwelling? But here's a rose;
Perhaps you slipped from its heart—who knows?

GITTIN' HOME.

Gittin' back to home ag'in, after all the strife,
The rattlin' an' the roarin' o' the busy city life;
Gittin' back to home ag'in—heart a-beatin' high,
Greener grows the meadows an' bluer is the sky!

World seems all dressed up fer it—neat as any pin!
Car wheels keep a-singin': " Gittin' home ag'in!"
Don't it please a feller when he's travelin' through
    the lan',
That home comes out to meet him an' takes him
    by the han'!

CHATTAHOOCHEE.

Sweet sings the Chattahoochee on its way toward
    the sea—
      The curling Chattahoochee,
      The whirling Chattahoochee—
And the mocking birds make answer to its music
    wild and free;
      The blue skies bend above it,
      The green hills lean and love it,
And the Chattahoochee singeth of the summer and
    the sea !

Sweet sings the Chattahoochee with radiant, rip-
    pled tides—
      The dreamy Chattahoochee,
      The gleamy Chattahoochee—
The Alabama hilltops from the Georgian it di-
    vides;

But floats this song above them :
" I lave them, and I love them ;
The green fields are my lovers, and the green hills
   are my brides ! "

Sweet sings the Chattahoochee to the east and to
   the west—
      The olden Chattahoochee,
      The golden Chattahoochee ;
But a secret in its bosom makes it love the sunset
   best ;
      For its soul seems ever sighing
      For a lost love unreplying,
When night steals from the mountains and is fold-
   ed to its breast.

Sweet sings the Chattahoochee of the passion of
   the past—
      The grieving Chattahoochee,
      Dream-weaving Chattahoochee,
And whatever be its secret still it holds—enfolds
   it fast ;

But when glooms the night above you,
Still that song: "I love you—love you!
And the sweetest rose that blossoms near my
bosom is the last!"

THE LOVE FEAST AT WAYCROSS.

It was in the town o' Waycross, not many weeks
 ago.
They had a big revival there, as like enough you
 know;
An' though many was converted an' fer pardon
 made to call,
Yet the Sunday mornin' love feast was the hap-
 piest time o' all !

'Twas a great experience meetin', an' it done me
 good to hear
The brotherin an' the sisterin that talked religion there;
You didn't have to ax 'em, ner coax 'em with a
 song;
Them people had religion, an' they told it right
 along !

Thar was one—a hard old sinner—'pears like I
　　knowed his name,
But I reckon I've fergot it—who to the altar
　　came;
An' he took the leader by the han', with beamin'
　　face an' bright,
An' said : "I'm comin' home, dear fren's; I'm
　　comin' home to-night ! "

Then a woman rose an' axed to be remembered in
　　their prayers :
" My husband's comin' home," said she, a-sheddin'
　　thankful tears ;
" I want you all to pray fer him; he's lived in
　　sin's control,
But I think the love o' Jesus is a-breakin' on his
　　soul ! "

Any shoutin'? Well, I reckon so ! One brother
　　give a shout :
Said he had so much religion he was 'bliged to let
　　it out !

An' the preacher jined the chorus, sayin' : "Brotherin, let 'er roll !
A man can't keep from shoutin' with religion in
his soul ! "

I tell you, 'twas a happy time; I wished 'twould
never end :
Each sinner in the church that day had Jesus fer a
friend ;
But a good old deacon said to 'em, while tears
stood in his eye :
" There's a better time 'an this, dear fren's,
a-comin' by an' by ! "

I hope some day those brotherin'll meet with one
accord
In the higher, holier love feast, whose leader is
the Lord ;
An' when this here life is over, with its sorrow an'
its sighs,
May the little church at Waycross jine the big
church in the skies !

A JUNE PASTORAL.

Fleecy clouds above you roll—
All the world's a tune
Thrillin' through a feller's soul,
Dreamin' here with June.

Butterflies with golden wings
Brush you—soft as silk,
While the poplar-shaded springs
Cool the buttermilk!

In the old fence corner—whew!
Melons—mind your tread!—
Where the sun is streamin' through
To their hearts o' red!

June she is—an' let her be!
June in fields an' towns;
Let her sweet lips stifle me,
While her honey drowns!

(157)

THE MOCKING BIRD.

He didn't know much music
  When first he come along ;
An' all the birds went wonderin'
  Why he didn't sing a song.

They primped their feathers in the sun,
  An' sung their sweetest notes ;
An' music jest come on the run
  From all their purty throats !

But still that bird was silent
  In summer time an' fall ;
He jest set still an' listened,
  An' he wouldn't sing at all !

But one night when them songsters
  Was tired out an' still,
An' the wind sighed down the valley
  An' went creepin' up the hill ;

When the stars was all a-tremble
  In the dreamin' fields o' blue,
An' the daisy in the darkness
  Felt the fallin' o' the dew ;

There come a sound o' melody
  No mortal ever heard,
An' all the birds seemed singin'
  From the throat o' one sweet bird !

Then the other birds went Mayin'
  In a land too fur to call ;
Fer there warn't no use in stayin'
  When one bird could sing fer all !

GOOD-BY.

There's a kind o' chilly feelin' in the blowin' o'
    the breeze,
An' a sense o' sadness stealin' through the tresses
    o' the trees ;
An' it's not the sad September that's slowly
    drawin' nigh,
But jest that I remember I'm here to say "Good-
    by ! "

"Good-by," the wind is wailin'; "good-by," the
    trees complain,
An' bend low down to whisper, with green leaves
    white with rain ;
"Good-by," the roses murmur, an' the bendin'
    lilies sigh,
As if they all felt sorry that I'm come to say
    "Good-by."

I reckon all have said it, some time or other—
    soft
An' easy like—with eyes low down, that couldn't
    look aloft
Fer the tears that trembled in 'em, fer the lips
    that choked the sigh
When it kind o' took holt o' the heart, an' made it
    beat " Good-by ! "

I didn't think 'twas hard to say, but standin' here
    alone,
With the pleasant past behin' me, an' the future all
    unknown,
A-gloomin' yonder in the dark, I can't keep back
    the sigh,
An' I'm weepin' like a woman as I tell you all
    " Good-by ! "

The work I've done is with you ; maybe some
    things went wrong,
Like a note that jars the music in the sweet flow
    of a song !

But, brethren, when you think o' me, I only ask
   you would
Say as the Master said o' one: "He's done jest
   what he could!"

An' when you sit together in the time that's goin'
   to be,
By your bright an' beamin' firesides in this
   pleasant land o' Lee,
Let the sweet past come before you, an' with
   somethin' like a sigh,
Jest say: "We ain't fergot him since the day he
   said ' Good-by ! ' "

A GEORGIA BARBECUE.

Faint wreaths of smoke are dreaming skyward in
    rings of blue ;
A subtle, savory steaming is softly filtered through
The sheltering trees that whisper the secret every-
    where,
While hill and valley revel in the dewed, delicious
    air !

And then, that crackle of the twigs above the
    smoky pits ;
Where brown and palatable pigs make Wisdom
    lose its wits !
And then—and then—the cry to arms ! Knives,
    forks, flash to and fro,
And hungry hundreds praise the Lord, from whom
    all blessings flow !

THE LAST INN.

This is the inn that I
   Have dreamed of all my days;
I enter—close the door—good-by!
   And the world may go its ways.
The soft, cool shadows round me creep;
I lay me down to rest—to sleep.

There is no reckoning here :
   Not any noise or strife ;
Nor shall one murmur to be where
   King Death is host to Life.
Still, curtained rest for ye that come,
But sightless eyes and lips made dumb.

Cold ice at head and feet,
   But flowers of colors grand
To make the air above you sweet
   And paint the roof of sand.

What more ?   And when the keen winds blow,
Sweet dreams in daisies 'neath the snow.

Good-night, friends, and farewell !
  Our lives must parted be ;
Grieve not that I with Death must dwell,
  For Death is kind to me.
Tired, I lay me down to rest,
A child lulled on a mother's breast.

THE EASTER BONNET.

Don't make 'em like they use to—done killed with
    too much style—
Fixed up with birds an' ribbons, till you know 'em
    half a mile:
They call 'em " Easter bonnets," in the big store
    windows hung—
Ain't nuthin' like the bonnets that they wore when
    we was young !

How much completer, sweeter, and neater was the
    old
Time bonnet, shadin' rosy cheeks an' ringlets
    black an' gold !
Plain, with no fixins on it—with a string o' red an'
    blue ;
But a kiss beneath that bonnet was as sweet as
    honey-dew !

Don't make 'em like they use to—done killed with
    too much style ;
An' yet—the girls that wear 'em give a feller sich
    a smile,
He kinder smooths it over—fergives 'em, so high-
    strung—
But they're nuthin' like the bonnets that they wore
    when we was young !

NOVEMBER NIGHTS.

November nights—November nights!
With all their rich and rare delights;
The blazing fire whose sparkling flames
Gleam with a lovelier light than Fame's!
Oh, heartful cheer! Oh, peaceful sights,
Walled in by cool November nights!

November nights—the stories told;
The lambs all gathered in the fold;
The flickering lights and shadows shed
O'er little ones tucked up in bed!
The mother's kiss—divine delights
That crown the sweet November nights!

November nights! the fiddler's feet
Keep time to music wild and sweet;
And every echoing rafter rings
Where Love each rosy partner swings!
Oh, rich are all the rare delights
That crown the cool November nights!

A TRAGEDY.

That's him there, on his coffin, in the cart,
  An' that's his wife a-creepin'
  In the crowd—'way off an' weepin';
Oh, the law is jest a-breakin' of her heart!

That's him there, on the scaffol'. See! he speaks;
  There's a woman there, a-holdin'
  Of the hands they'll soon be foldin',
An' the tears is jest a-rainin' down her cheeks.

That's him there in the coffin lyin' low,
  An' the woman—first to love him
  An' the last to bend above him,
Is his mother—but I reckon you would know!

SOME THOUGHTS OF LEE.

How's all the boys down there in Lee—Joe John-
 son an' Doc Brown?
When I think o' them, it 'pears to me the rain's
 a-comin' down;
Or, it may be that the distance makes a haze aroun'
 my eyes—
Fer the sunshine's kind o' blindin' when it comes
 from them old skies!

How's all the boys down there in Lee? I guess
 they're livin' still,
Fer I seem to hear 'em singin' down the road to
 Wells' mill,
Where the water made sich music in the sweet an'
 old-time years;
(I think I hear it drippin'—but I guess it's jest my
 tears!)

How's all the boys down there in Lee? I guess
   they've 'bout fergot
A feller what is gone away an' kinder changed his lot;
But yet he ain't fergot 'em—wherever he may be
He'll always hear, in music clear, the far-off bells
   o' Lee!

The bells that used to ring fer us at early mornin'
   light;
The bells that used to sing fer us—soft in our
   dreams at night;
The dear old bells! What organ swells one half
   as sweet to me
As jest their "tinkle, tinkle" in the meadowy lands
   o' Lee!

But this isn't what I mean to say: How's all the
   boys down there?
I guess the frosts o' life has shed the silver on
   their hair—
Or, it may be that the distance makes a haze aroun'
   my eyes,
Fer the sunshine's kind o' blindin' when it comes
   from them old skies!

THE CHAP IN THE BRANCH.

You may talk about your pleasures o' the summer
time, an' sich,
An' jest pile your money measures till the people
say you're rich ;
Take a trip off to the seashore, from your swel-
terin' city ranch,
But—the chap that has the most fun is a-wadin' in
the branch !

You may kinder slip the weather by a trip acrost
the sea,
An' feel the salty blowin' o' the breezes brisk an'
free,
An' pay some other feller fer conductin' o' the
ranch,
But—the chap that keeps the coolest is a-wadin'
in the branch !

Jest take a look an' see him : his feet is bare an'
  flat ;
Suspenders made o' cotton, an' him wearin' *one* at
  that !
His hat brim torn an' hangin' !—jest keep your
  city ranch—
The pictur' that's the brighest is the pictur' in the
  branch !

THE SONGS OF THE WIND.

How sings the wind in the splendid day
' When the world is wild with the wealth of May?

" The world is thrilling with light and love—
There was never a cloud in the heavens above:
Never a mateless and moaning dove!
Never a grave for a rose to hide,
And never a rose that died! "

How sings the wind in the hopeless night
When the lone, long winters are cold and white?

" There are rainbows back of the storms to be—
Back of the storms and their mystery ;
But oh, for the ships that are lost at sea !
And oh, for the love in the lonesome lands,
Far from the clasp of the drowning hands ! "

So the wind singeth: Its God decrees
The wind should sing such songs as these—
Should laugh in the sunlight's silver waves
And toss the green on the world's sad graves.
But why, in the night, should it sing to me
Of the ships—the ships that are lost at sea?

THE RAINBOW.

Flash, storm, your lightnings from their sheath,
  While bolt on bolt is hurled ;
Of your great wrath God makes a wreath
  Of glory round the world !

(176)

THE WORD HE DIDN'T SAY.

When we went to camp meetin' I had a word to
 say,
But I kept a-pullin' roses—like they all was in the
 way !
An' I did say : " Here's a red 'un ! an' this vi'let—
 ain't it blue ? "
But what I wanted most to say was—" ain't as
 sweet as you ! "

I recollect, 'twas rainin';—no, 'pears like the *sun*
 was out,
Fer I seen your curls a-shinin' on your neck an'
 round about ;
An' the moon was—no she *wasn't !*—don't think
 the moon had riz !
(When a feller's got a sweetheart, don't she turn
 that head o' his ?)

When we went to camp meetin'—here goes! I had
    a word
To say to you, and that was jest the one that
    wasn't heard !
But since you ain't here listenin', with them bright
    curls 'round your brow,
I'll say, I loved you ! an'—an'—an' I'm lovin' of
    you *now !*

THE WHIP–POOR–WILL.

That was the song ! We heard it years ago—
  Hark ! from the wiry brambles and the deep,
  Dark woods, and where the valley's violets sleep,
The curt, cool notes, melodiously flow !
That was the song ! In many a nest I know
  The birds are cuddled, and the clear skies weep
  Upon the morning-glories ; shadows creep
Over the hollows where the hushed streams flow.

That song ! that song ! and still your hand in mine,
  And still your true heart beating near my own !
  And still the vines—the place—the garden
    still !
Dear heart, I love you ! Let your lips incline—
  The lips whose roses bloom for me alone
  As blooms the same song of the whip-poor-will !

(179)

HUNT HIM DOWN.

Ho! good people of every town,
Here is a brother : hunt him down !
Roar at his heels like a raging flood—
Slake your thirst with his heart's red blood ;
For he was tempted—he sinned, he fell
From heights of heaven to depths of hell!
Fugitive—fleeing the saintly town,
Hunt him down !   Hunt him down !

Ho ! good people of every town,
Sage and sinner and knave and clown,
Swell the ranks with their storm and strife
In the maddening race for a human life !
Pause not ye for his gasp and groan—
Aim the arrow and hurl the stone !
Past the village and through the town
Hunt him down !   Hunt him down !

Care not ye for the grief he feels ;
Let the bloodhounds howl at his burning heels;
Let the cold, sharp stones of the cruel street
Pierce the wounds in his bleeding feet !
Hurl your hisses and block his way,
Till he stands at last like a beast at bay !
Search the village and sack the town—
Hunt him down !   Hunt him down !

Ho ! good people of every town,
Let not mercy your justice drown ;
'Tis human game—'tis a soul in woe,
Whose white Redeemer died long ago !
Scourge him—slay him ! 'tis little loss :
A sinner clings to the crimson cross,
Asking not for your shining crown,
Dead in the darkness—hunted down !

CLOSE TO SPRINGTIME.

Gittin' close to springtime—know it by the way
The sun is streamin', gleamin' in the middle o' the
    day ;
Know it by the river that is lazyin' along,
An' the mocking birds a-primpin' o' their feathers
    fer a song !

Gittin' close to springtime—know it by the signs,
Hear it in the whisper o' the maples an' the pines ;
Feel it in the blowin' o' the breezes, singin' sweet ;
See it in the daisies jest a-dreamin' at my feet !

Gittin' close to springtime ; hope she'll come to
    stay ;
Got a million kisses fer the red lips o' the May !
Wearyin' to meet her—list'nin' all the time
Fer the tinkle o' her footsteps—her roses an' her
    rhyme !

A SONG OF MYSTERIES.

Who shall say what snowflakes light
Falling on the lambs at night,
Clothed them in their coats of white?
Who shall say what veins of sun
Through the rose's petals run,
Till they crimson, one by one?
This, O Heart, is all our knowing:
Lambs are clad and flowers are blowing.

When the wild birds are a-wing
In the blue and bloom of spring,
Who shall say what makes them sing?
Who shall tell this heart of mine
Why in thunder and in shine
Still the mossed-oak lures the vine?
We but know the wild bird singeth
And the lured vine clingeth, clingeth.

Who shall say why rosiest dawn
Gleameth, streameth, dreameth on,
To the breast of Darkness drawn?
And why thou, by earth caressed,
Still hath sought me—loved me best,
Crept like sunlight to my breast?
Day and Dark may love and sever,
But thou lovest me forever!

MARY, AFTER CALVARY.

In the night when they scourged Him and crowned
    Him
  With thorns that were sharp as their spears,
They struck my white arms from around Him
  And fast fell my tears.

And weeping and following slowly—
  They mocking my love and my loss,
Knew not that my lips leaning lowly
  Kissed His steps to the cross!

They knew not my down-streaming tresses,
  With myrrh and with spikenard made sweet,
Had covered with golden caresses
  His beautiful feet!

So, weeping, I followed my Master
  Till the cross was laid wearily down,

And the night in the heavens gloomed faster
    On Calvary's crown.

And there—as He rested Him, weary,
    My love knew its sweetest reward—
For His lips seemed to speak to me: "Mary!"
    My name from my Lord!

No crown of sharp thorns did I weave Him
    To crimson His forehead of white;
The last in the darkness to leave Him,
    The first in the light!

For there, at the gates of His prison,
    Faith freed from doubt's darkened control,
I knew that my Master was risen
    And joy filled my soul!

He liveth!   No more am I weeping,
    But still, where God's angels are fair,
My love to His footstool is creeping
    And He smiles on me there!

WEARY THE WAITING.

There's an end to all toiling some day—sweet
    day,
  But it's weary the waiting, weary!
There's a harbor somewhere in a peaceful bay
Where the sails will be furled and the ship will
    stay
At anchor—somewhere in the far-away—
  But it's weary the waiting, weary!

There's an end to the troubles of souls opprest,
  But it's weary the waiting, weary!
Some time in the future when God thinks best
He'll lay us tenderly down to rest,
And roses 'll bloom from the thorns in the breast—
  But it's weary the waiting, weary!

There's an end to the world with its stormy frown,
  But it's weary the waiting, weary!

There's a light somewhere that no dark can
    drown,
And where life's sad burdens are all laid down,
A crown—thank God!—for each cross—a crown!
    But it's weary the waiting, weary!

JONES'S COTTON PLANTER.

He ain't of no account at all, jest give up ever'-
    thing
Fer what he calls "inventin'," been a-foolin' 'long
    sence spring
With a queer kind o' contraption which has turned
    that head o' his;
Calls it "Jones's Cotton Planter," but the Lord
    knows *what* it is!

He took it to the city, showed it to the board o'
    trade,
An' they thought it was amazin' an' said: "Jones,
    your fortun's made!"
I know they was a-foolin' him—got lots o' imper-
    dence!
But he come home highfalutin', an' he hain't
    knowed nuthin' sence.

He's built himself a blacksmith shop, an' there he
    works away,
With the pesky bellows roarin' like a cyclone night
    an' day;
Ain't reg'lar at his meals no more, man of a fam'ly,
    too;
I wish that cotton planter was in — Halifax,
    I do!

It strikes me they've got things enough without
    his makin' more,
Unless he fixed up somethin' fer the grass that's at
    his door;
But the cotton planter's got him, an' the children's
    worked to death,
Fer he keeps 'em at the bellows till they're almost
    out o' breath.

Sich a blowin', sich a hammerin', sich a sawin'—
    never stops;
Can't git him interested in the weather or the
    crops.

"I'm a-gittin' there!" he'll tell you; "she'll be
  ready by the fall;
And Jones's cotton planter'll take the shine from
  off 'em all!"

He's done fur. No use talkin'; he's a ruint man
  as sure
As Betsy, there, is sittin' with her knittin' at the
  door;
Alas! fer all the children—they'll be down to skin
  an' bones,
An' Jones's cotton planter'll be the epitaph o'
  Jones!

HAPPY LAN'.

Three niggers with a banjer—it's fun to hear 'em
sing—
A rattlin' off the music on a knotted fiddle-
string
Acrost a old cigar box—they're happy on the
way,
An' they make " The Suwanee River " sing a song
to " Nellie Gray ! "

" With a plink, plank, plunk,
An' it's happy lan'
Whar you doan give a nickel
Fer a po' white man ! "

Three niggers with a banjer—they're makin' music
fine ;
Jes' done a-choppin' cotton, where the white man
had 'em gwine !

Doan care how corn's a-sellin'—be watermillions
  soon,
An' that's why they're a-yellin' to the old plantation tune—

    " With a plink, plank, plunk,
      An' it's happy lan'
      Whar you doan give a nickel
      Fer a po' white man ! "

Three niggers with a banjer—talk 'bout the " Sunny South,"
They sing like watermillions was a-meltin' in their
  mouth ;
Jest happy as three blackbirds six miles from any
  trap :
" Oh, when yo' foot strike Zion yo' hat rim go
  ker-flap ! "

    " With a plink, plank, plunk,
      An' it's happy lan'
      Whar you doan give a nickel
      Fer a po' white man ! "

LET MISS LINDY PASS.

Lizard on de fence rail,
  Blacksnake in de grass ;
Rabbit in de brier-patch—
  Oh, let Miss Lindy pass!

  Let Miss Lindy pass—
  Her foot won't ben' de grass ;
  Rabbit, lizard, blacksnake,
  Oh, let Miss Lindy pass.

Squirrel in de co'nfiel',
  Eat yo' br'akfas' fas' ;
Set up straight an' watch de gate
  An' let Miss Lindy pass.

  Let Miss Lindy pass,
  Lak' de sunshine on de grass!
  Set up straight an' watch de gate
  An' let Miss Lindy pass.

White rose in de gyarden walk,
 Wid a dewdrap lookin'-glass,
Bresh dat dew fum off'en you
 An' let Miss Lindy pass.

  Let Miss Lindy pass,
  An' she'll pin you on at las';
  De goodness knows she's de sweetes' rose—
  So let Miss Lindy pass!

A CHEAT!

O April, you your skies may arch,
    But you're a cheat—no doubt ;
You stole the blustering winds o' March
    To blow your curls about !

TO A LITTLE FELLOW.

Ho ! little fellow—how d'ye do ?
Long time since I have looked on you !
But I know your eyes are the same bright blue—
April eyes, where the sun slips through :
Ho ! little fellow—how d'ye do ?

Ho ! little fellow—how d'ye do ?
Seem to feel, as I sit an' view
Your picture, there on the mantel shelf,
The arms, the charms of your own dear self !
For you kissed me oft, and you loved me true :
Ho ! little fellow—how d'ye do ?

Ho ! little fellow—how d'ye do ?
Same little fellow that once I knew ?
Never a change for all the years—
Same sweet laughter and same bright tears ?

Oh, for a word from the lips of you !
Ho ! little fellow—how d'ye do ?

Ho ! little fellow—far away !
Dream, some time, of the words I say,
When the dark drifts over your eyes of blue,
And the angels look through the lace at you !
Dream that I love you ; but love me, too !
Ho ! little fellow—how d'ye do ?

A SONG.

Sweetheart, there is no splendor
  In all God's splendid skies
Bright as the lovelight tender
  That dwells in thy dear eyes!

Sweetheart, there are no blisses
  Like those thy lips distil ;
Of all the world's sweet kisses
  Thy kiss is sweetest still!

Sweetheart, no white dove flying
  Had e'er as soft a breast
As this sweet hand that's lying
  Clasped in my own—at rest!

Sweetheart, there is no glory
  That clusters 'round my life
Bright as this bright, sweet story:
  " My sweetheart and my wife ! "

MY GIFTS.

Give not to me life's splendors—they would blind
  The eyes that now have light to see the way ;
  Only a little sunlight for my day,
And for my night the shadows soft and kind ;
And for my wealth the quiet of the mind,
  Gentle and sweet ; and lips that sing or say
  In kindness, and are answered when they pray ;
And for my glory duty, love-defined.
And give to me the love of her whose kiss
  Is recompense for toil ; whose smiles await
My coming, brightening with expected bliss
  In some sweet spot where twilight lingereth
    late ;
And yet one other blessing crowning this,
  In little footsteps pattering to the gate !

A LITTLE BOOK.

[Charles Warren Stoddard's South Sea Idyls.]

A little book with here and there a leaf
  Turned at some tender passage ; how it seems
  To speak to me—to fill my soul with dreams
Sweet as first love, and beautiful though brief !
Here was her glory ; on this page her grief—
  For tears have stained it ; here the sunlight
      streams,
  And there the stars withheld from her their
      beams
And sorrow sought her white soul like a thief !
And here her name, and as I breathe the sweet,
  Soft syllables, a presence in the room
    Sheds a rare radiance ; but I may not look :
The yellowed leaves are fluttering at my feet ;
  The light is gone, and I—lost in the gloom,
  Weep like a woman o'er this little book.

SAINT MICHAEL'S BELLS.

I wonder if the bells ring now, as in the days of
   old,
From the solemn star-crowned tower with the
   glittering cross of gold ;
The tower that overlooks the sea whose shining
   bosom swells
To the ringing and the singing of sweet Saint
   Michael's bells ?

I have heard them in the morning when the mists
   gloomed cold and gray
O'er the distant walls of Sumter looking seaward
   from the bay,
And at twilight I have listened to the musical
   farewells
That came flying, sighing, dying from sweet Saint
   Michael's bells.

Great joy it was to hear them, for they sang sweet
    songs to me
Where the sheltered ships rocked gently in the
    haven—safe from sea,
And the captains and the sailors heard no more
    the ocean's knells,
But thanked God for home and loved ones and
    sweet Saint Michael's bells.

They seemed to waft a welcome across the ocean's
    foam
To all the lost and lonely: "Come home—come
    home—come home!
Come home, where skies are brighter—where love
    still yearning dwells!"
So sang the bells in music—the sweet Saint
    Michael's bells!

They are ringing now as ever. But I know that
    not for me
Shall the bells of sweet Saint Michael's ring wel-
    come o'er the sea;

I have knelt within their shadow, where my heart
 still dreams and dwells,
But I'll hear no more the music of sweet Saint
 Michael's bells.

Oh, ring, sweet bells, forever, an echo in my
 breast
Soft as a mother's voice that lulls a loved one into
 rest !
Ring welcome to the hearts at home—to me your
 sad farewells
When I sleep the last sleep, dreaming of sweet
 Saint Michael's bells !

SONG.

Love is folly, Love is hate—
   Let us dwell with Love :
He's a churl of low estate—
   He's a God above !
Piping robin—moaning dove—
Loved because his name is Love .

If he hath a garden spot—
   Dwelling in the light ;
If he hath a savage cot,
   Covered by the night ;—
We must love in praise or blame,
Since sweet Love's his name—his name !

MAID O' THE MIST.

Are you watching the ships sailing southward,
　O mystical Maid o' the Mist ?
Do you wave your white hand
When they're nearing the land—
　Are the tips of your white fingers kissed
To the captains and sailors who shout o'er the
　　foam
For joy of the lights in the harbor at home ?

Are you watching the ships sailing southward,
　O beautiful Maid o' the Mist ?
When the waves on the bars
Make their moan to the stars,
　Do you keep with the night winds a tryst ?
The watch fires are dead on the desolate strand
And darkness hath hidden thy beckoning hand.

You are watching the ships sailing southward,
O Maid o' the Mist ! but I know
That the pitiful waves
Never tell of the graves
Fathoms and fathoms below ;
And the winds that blow inland o'er sea and o'er
sound
In mercy have stifled the cries of the drowned !

A SONG OF SHIPS.

The sky made a whip o' the winds and lashed the
    sea into foam,
And the keen blowing gales tore the flags and the
    sails of the ships that were plunging home;
Of the ships that were tossing home on the black
    and billowy deep,
But who shall reach to the wrecks, the wrecks,
    where the ships and their captains sleep?

    Oh, wrecks by the black seas tossed,
      In the desolate ocean nights!
    Lost, lost in the darkness! Lost
      In sight o' the harbor lights!

The sky made a veil o' the clouds and a scourge o'
    the lightning red,
And the blasts bowed the masts of the ships that
    fared where love and the sea gulls led;

Of the ships that were faring home with love for
   the waiting breast,
But where is the love that can reach to the wrecks
   where the ships and their captains rest?

   Oh, ships of our love, wave-tossed,
      In the fathomless ocean nights!
   Lost, lost in the blackness! Lost
      In sight o' the harbor lights!

There was once a ship of my soul that tossed on a
   stormy sea,
And this was my prayer when the nights gloomed
   drear: " Send my soul's ship safe to me!
Send my soul's ship safely home from billows and
   blackened skies!"
But where is the soul that can reach to the depths,
   the depths where my soul's ship lies?

   Oh, ship of my soul, storm-tossed
      In the far and the fearful nights!
   Lost, lost, in the blackness! Lost
      In sight o' the harbor lights!

HER BEAUTIFUL HANDS.

God's roses are sweet and His lilies are fair,
  As they bend 'neath the dews from above;
They are splendid and fair—but they can not com-
  pare
  With the beautiful hands of my love.
No jewels adorn them—no glittering bands—
They are just as God made them, these sweet,
  sweet hands!

And not for earth's gems, or its bright diadems,
  Or the pearls from the depths of the sea,
Or the queens of the lands with their beautiful
  hands
Should these dear hands be taken from me.
What exquisite blisses await their commands!
They were made for my kisses, these dear, sweet
  hands.

Ay, made for my kisses! And when, some day,
  My life shall be robbed of its trust,
And the lips that are colder shall kiss them away
  And hide them in daisies and dust;
I will kneel in the dark where the angel stands
And my kiss shall be last on these dear, sweet
  hands.

TO THE NEW YEAR.

One song for thee, New Year,
One universal prayer :
Teach us—all other teaching far above—
To hide dark Hate beneath the wings of Love;
To slay all hatred, strife,
And live the larger life!
To bind the wounds that bleed :
　To lift the fallen, lead the blind
As only Love can lead—
　To live for all mankind!

Teach us, New Year, to be
Free men among the free,
Our only master Duty ; with no God
Save one—our Maker ; monarchs of the sod!
Teach us, with all its might,
Its darkness and its light ;

Its heart-beats tremulous,
  Its grief, its gloom,
  Its beauty and its bloom—
God made the world for us!

THE MASTER'S COMING.

In a desolate Night and lonely, afar in a desolate
    land,
I waited the Master's coming—the touch of His
    healing hand.
The gates of His house were guarded and sealed
    with a seal of stone,
Yet still for His steps I waited and wept in the
    dark alone.

And I said : " When the guards are dreaming I will
    steal to His couch of rest ;
He will think of my weary vigils and welcome me
    to His breast."
But lo ! when the seal was broken, the couch where
    my Master lay
Held only His shining raiment—they had taken
    my Lord away !

Then my soul in its grief and anguish lay down in
the dark to die
Under a hopeless heaven, under a sunless sky;
But my dreams were all of the Master—dear as
my soul was dear,
And waking, I saw the glory of His beautiful Presence there !

And He said, as I fell and worshiped: "Arise,
and the Master see;
Behold the thorns that have crowned Him—the
wounds that were made for thee!"

.   .   .   .

I wait for the Master's coming now as in days
gone by,
Under a hopeful heaven, under a cloudless sky;
And still when the guards are dreaming I steal to
His couch of rest;
His smile through the darkness lightens, and wel-
comes me to His breast !

A SONG OF LIBERTY.

Across the land from strand to strand
  Loud ring the bugle notes,
And Freedom's smile from isle to isle,
  Like Freedom's banner floats.

The velvet vales sing "Liberty!"
  To answering skies serene;
The mountains, sloping to the sea,
  Wave all their flags of green.

The rivers, dashing to the deep,
  Still echo loud and long,
And all their waves in glory leap
  To one immortal song.

One song of Liberty and Life
  That was and is to be,
Till tyrant flags are trampled rags
  And all the world is free!

One song—the nations hail the notes
   From sounding sea to sea,
And answer from their thrilling throats
   That song of Liberty !

They answer and an echo comes
   From chained and troubled isles,
And roars like ocean's thunder-drums
   Where glad Columbia smiles.

Where, crowned and great, she sits in state
   Beneath her flag of stars,
Her heroes' blood the sacred flood
   That crimsoned all its bars !

Hail to our Country ! strong she stands,
   Nor fears the war drum's beat ;
The sword of Freedom in her hands—
   The tyrant at her feet !

(12)

THE END.